A WORLD RULED BY MICE

A WORLD RULED BY MICE

JOHN PHELPS

Matador
9 Priory Business Park,
Wistow Road, Kibworth Beauchamp,
Leicestershire. LE8 0RX
Tel: 0116 279 2299
Email: books@troubador.co.uk
Web: www.troubador.co.uk/matador
Twitter: @matadorbooks

ISBN 978 1800465 480

British Library Cataloguing in Publication Data.
A catalogue record for this book is available from the British Library.

Printed and bound in Great Britain by 4edge Limited
Typeset in 11pt Minion Pro by Troubador Publishing Ltd, Leicester, UK

Matador is an imprint of Troubador Publishing Ltd

Dedicated to my late father Gilbert Phelps, my late sister
Jean Lawson and my wife Derri.

CHAPTER 1

"Is he the right rodent for the job?" the executives' conference was asked once more.

The charismatic Caxton stroked his whiskers and pondered. A decision had to be taken on Marcus's suitability, or otherwise, and what the other options might be.

"I have a major fashion feature to prepare, not to mention a possible interview with Polo," Phaedra, the Features Editor, said hurriedly.

Adonis, the Sports Editor, took his eyes off Phaedra for one moment to join the discussion. "As you know, I have commitments, too… both on and off the field."

"And I have plenty on my plate as well, especially with the elections round the corner," Titus, the Chief Reporter, added.

"Me, too," said Iago, the Deputy Editor, whose remit included ensuring that all news coverage in particular was up to scratch. He was very much a details mouse.

Caxton, who noticed that the latter had gone puce as he spoke, greeted all the observations with one of his famed smiles. It was the sort of smile that rendered minions captivated and cowed at the same time. He was well aware that Iago had been the prime doubter of the choice of Marcus... and that he now wished he had not raised these doubts lest the assignment be given to him instead.

"We'd better wheel him in," he said with a nod towards Helen, his secretary.

Marcus was sitting disconsolately in his corner near a window in the *Phoenix Standard* newsroom. He knew he had put his neck on the line but, although filled with misgivings, felt that, on balance, he had made the right move. It was potentially his chance to shine, and his fate was now in the paws of the hierarchy.

The newsroom was almost deserted. The news desk telephone was manned by Gertrude, Titus's secretary, and the others present were three chatty young reporters and, of course, Cicero, who, once more, was engaged in his research into 'The Origins of Mousekind'.

The telephone had been ringing incessantly, and Gertrude had just asked the reporters to keep the noise down so that she could concentrate on dealing with the calls. The reporters were now debating in whispers the likely outcome of the latest football fixture between the town team and the Trojans. The topic was, inevitably perhaps, putting the election in the shade.

Marcus looked up nervously when he saw Helen approaching him. "His Nibs wants words with you," she told him, before turning and motioning him to follow.

All eyes were on him as he entered Caxton's opulent office. Marcus was aware of all the gazes, especially the one that actually counted.

"Come into my lair and take a pew," the Editor said with a basilisk beam. Marcus took the one seat that was available.

It was in the middle of the curved row of minions who sat facing the Editor's desk and within two feet of the great mouse himself.

"This is quite an undertaking you're asking to take on," the Editor added once Marcus had sat down. "Are you sure you feel up to it?"

"Yes, of course," Marcus answered, feeling anything but sure. "If I didn't think I could do it, I wouldn't have put my name forward."

The basilisk beam grew even brighter.

"Right! That's all I want to know!" said Caxton. "You are aware of the hazards, or at least of the hazards we know about, and you appreciate that there could be other hazards that unexpectedly present themselves." A pause followed, during which Caxton gazed into Marcus's eyes. The beam then returned.

Marcus experienced a feeling of elation when he heard the words: "You've got the job, well done!"

"Thank you. I will do my best not to let you down," he said.

"Of course you won't. We trust you implicitly," he was told. He knew failure was not an option, in any case.

The punctilious Iago was the next to speak. "Before you go, Phaedra will need to interview you for the potboiler. She will, of course, be looking for an angle." Phaedra nodded before Iago turned to ask her: "Have you been able to pin down the elusive Polo yet?"

Helen replied: "No, but I haven't given up yet."

"And indeed, you mustn't!" Caxton roared. "We have got to get him before the 'Troy Courier' does. Remember, he lives exactly the same distance away from us and Troy, and it's imperative for us to be first!"

The room went silent for a while before Titus said: "I believe Polo's team is to include a gerbil and a hamster."

"That's right," said Adonis. "One is known for his resourcefulness and the other for his strength. The hamster is almost as strong as I am and can be relied upon to carry lots of baggage."

"Steady on!" Caxton boomed. "You're in danger of talking yourself on to the trip!" Adonis winced while the others fell about laughing. The mighty six foot five Sports Editor was known in equal measure for his mighty muscles and his propensity to self-pamper.

"Never mind!" Caxton added. "We have got our own mouse on the expedition, which, as far as we know, is more than the 'Courier' has. Let me know if the situation changes, of course."

Caxton then turned to Marcus and eyed him intently before saying: "I should imagine you've got some planning and packing to do. Let me know when exactly you will be setting off, and, of course, tell us if there's anything you need from the *Standard*."

Marcus mumbled his thanks and, knowing his presence was no longer required, made his way to the door and returned to his workstation.

His heart was beating furiously because he had acted out of character. Although of above average height, at six feet tall, he had been berated for failing to make his presence felt, to be assertive. As a result, other mice of smaller stature – and, on occasions, less talent – had left him behind in the never-ending quest for ascendancy. At the top of the tree, by a considerable distance, of course, was Caxton, another six-footer, who had the knack of appearing several inches taller.

Now Marcus was all set to join forces with the iconic but enigmatic Polo and take part in a potentially historic event. Along with Caxton, the inventor Da Vinci and the current Prime Minister, Polo was one of the leading pillars of the community on the Isle of Andronicus.

Marcus had yet to meet Polo, although he had heard plenty. He had heard plenty, too, about the unexplored parts of the massive island. Much of it was inevitably speculation, as no one really knew what to expect when attempting to set foot in these parts. All he knew for sure was that the experience was going to be life-changing… although he had no idea how or to what extent.

CHAPTER 2

Mountainous waves crashing into monolithic cliffs surrounded the Isle of Andronicus. The island itself was reckoned to occupy close to three million acres. The waves could, and often did, rise to a height of a thousand feet or more everywhere. Dark coastal clouds and mists were ever present, making shoreline visibility almost non-existent and rendering any notion of trying to leave the island by boat sheer madness.

It was as if some superpowered force from under the seabed had driven a vast tract of land skywards and left it towering over everything that surrounded it.

The island's inhabitants experienced four distinct seasons that massively influenced lifestyles. The seasons were Temperate, Cold, Wet and Hot. The Temperate Season was six months long, while the other three took up two months each.

Not surprisingly, most of the above-ground activities and social occasions occurred while the climate was temperate. Moving around became increasingly easy once the Temperate Season started. It was the season in which

Marcus was to join Polo's expedition into the unknown, and it was seen as the time for grasping opportunities. It was a time when the weather patterns could change with little warning but without extremes. Rain and sunshine could appear unexpectedly, and temperatures could go up and down, but although the changes could cause discomfort and inconvenience at times, they were rarely life-threatening.

That would all change at the end of six months, when a blast of icy air would give notice that the Cold Season was on its way.

Within forty-eight hours, the temperature would then plummet to forty degrees below zero or lower, and most of the Andronicus inhabitants would retreat to the burrows that led to their underground homes. The burrows, featuring shops, offices and a host of other facilities, had been designed and created over a period of many years to form a subterranean metropolis. Such a metropolis would be a feature of Troy and Carthage, as well as Phoenix. Town mice and some other forms of life could now find sanctuary from the elements that were mainly dominated by blizzards.

Inhabitants living outside these towns had to retreat to individual burrows or make their way to an urban guest suite… one of the many concepts that could be attributed to Da Vinci.

The Cold Season tended to end as abruptly as it had begun. The blizzards would die down and, again almost without warning, give way to the Wet Season.

When its time came, an azure blue sky, featuring not even a speck, would be taken over and monopolised by a single black cloud that only allowed glimpses of blue to appear on the periphery. The cloud exuded menace, and it was not long before sheets of lightning illuminated almost every corner of the island. Deafening thunderclaps followed, and the rain cascaded down like a series of monumental waterfalls. Streams turned into rivers, rivers became raging lakes and parched parcels of land disappeared under towering banks of moving water. No wonder nearly all the above-ground houses had been built on sturdy stilts. The houses then served as havens for those who chose to remain above ground until the floods started to subside, and it became possible to move around by boat and eventually by buggy or on foot.

As the season neared its end, the winds would drop, the skies would clear and the monsoon-like rains would turn into intermittent showers. Excess water would find its way into lakes, rivers and waterfalls that cascaded down cliffs.

It would then be time for the Hot Season, during which temperatures would rise to fifty degrees or more during the day and drop to around fifteen at night. Strong winds, that could occasionally reach hurricane force, would keep most inhabitants underground during the day and bring with them the constant threat of causing fires to rage out of control, severely damage vegetation and decimate crops. The island's Chief Harvest Mouse found these times challenging but did his best to keep damage to a minimum.

The season's arrival would be heralded by a tumultuous tremor. The island would shake like an infant being disciplined by an overbearing parent, before a plume or larva could be seen shooting into the air on the horizon. Inhabitants were made to gasp for breath.

One advantage that the Andronicus climate did offer was its predictability. The islanders had, over the years, learned to adapt and plan in advance. Homes, designed by Da Vinci and those in his employ, had been created accordingly. Towns tended to be near the coast, where running water could be harnessed to generate electricity. The much-venerated Da Vinci was behind this, too, of course.

Da Vinci, Caxton and Aristotle, the current Prime Minister, possessed most of the power and influence over other mice. The mice minions, in turn, enjoyed superiority over all the other islanders. Gerbils, hamsters and other rodents were subservient to them, and they were superior to the remaining inhabitants… especially cats.

Mouse and cat games, organised by Adonis among others, were especially popular as a leisure activity. They would be held in either Phoenix or Troy and would attract crowds from far and wide. The biggest fans of all were the harvest mice, who tended to lord it over giant farms where wheat, maize and barley fields abounded and from where grain growers could bring in their produce as well as enjoy their favourite sport.

Other farmers specialised in dairy products, with demand for milk strong and for cheese bordering on manic. However, the goats were just two feet tall, and the cows stood at a height of just six inches at most. This meant that large herds were needed to maximise profits. The sight of a cow or goat herd being driven into and through town was widely recognised as a counter-attraction to the mouse and cat games.

All these activities took place on parts of the island that were habitable. The centre of Andronicus was taken up by a swathe of desert land that exceeded the size of what used to be the United Kingdom. In the centre of that swathe was an area known as The Oven, which featured a climate so unforgiving that it remained largely untouched by even the Temperate Season. Sandstorms and baking heat dominated there, and even Polo had abandoned attempts to explore The Oven. Storms had driven him back on three separate occasions, and the great explorer had been compelled, for the time being, at least, to admit defeat.

At the moment, Polo's focus was on the island's northern region, which, because of the unpredictability of conditions, was considered to be even more hazardous than The Oven.

Storms could sweep the region without warning. Temperatures at such times could almost match those that prevailed at The Oven, or they could easily be twenty degrees below zero… or something in-between. The weather could be hot, cold, wet or dry, at any given time. The terrain could be changeable, too. It could be stony at one moment and muddy the next. Undulating hills could suddenly become mountains before the ground flattened out again. Deep crevices lay in wait for anyone who might be unwary for just one second. And on top of all this was the need to watch out for scorpions, snakes and giant spiders. The region had become known as the Domain of the Devil.

Many islanders questioned Polo's sanity, on hearing how he wanted to explore it. They heard that one of the reasons he did was simply because 'it was there'. Another was the rumour, based purely on hearsay, that the Domain of the Devil harboured unimaginable riches. What exactly those riches were, where and in what quantity they could be found, was anyone's guess. This was a question that fascinated many, perhaps because most of the island's wealth came in the forms of cheese and grain and, from time to time, whatever the waves threw up. With the latter in mind, the more agile mice were able to gain kudos by clambering down parts of cliffs to caves that could be found halfway down. Some of the caves contained pools, where crabs, lobsters, various fish and occasional shoals of whales could be found. All these were much sought after and regarded as dinner-table delicacies. Especially valued were the minute whales, which, when served by the score on a plate, were the biggest delight for diners. One reason the whales were so sought after was that, like the mice, they were mammals. And one of the favourite topics of after-dinner conversation was why mammals differed so much in size, shape and other ways.

CHAPTER 3

It was almost time to go. Marcus made sure his electric-powered buggy was properly charged once more and then, yet again, checked that he had everything he thought he needed. Polo had advised him to bring plenty of water, cheese, sun cream and waterproof clothing. The great explorer had warned him in no uncertain terms that much of the expedition would be into the unknown and that preparing for every conceivable eventuality would not be possible. Such a warning would have normally deterred someone as unadventurous as Marcus, but this was different.

His timidity had concealed an underlying desire to do well in at least something. He craved success and respect in equal measure. He was weary of being known as a stick-in-the-mud and felt wounded by the number of times he had been passed over and overtaken by younger mice whenever a chance of advancement at the *Standard* had cropped up.

Marcus had joined the staff at the newspaper as a cub reporter just over fifteen years ago. His capacity for hard work and willingness to put in more hours than any of his colleagues had been noted by the hierarchy, and his reward had been a steadily increasing workload and nothing else. The then News Editor/Chief Reporter had urged him to be more assertive – on the telephone, in the field and in the office, too – but to no avail. His failure to be assertive had for years been a source of irritation, even contempt, among his superiors and one of amusement among others. Some of his younger colleagues had inevitably taken note and jockeyed themselves into situations in which they would be singled out for kudos while Marcus would be earmarked for the more wearing, unrewarding tasks.

The prospect of joining an expedition that was likely to be fraught with danger was not relished in the newsroom and, in any case, there were other assignments to be tackled. Apart from the forthcoming elections, there were various sporting events, the trial of a suspected serial killer and interviews with various celebrities. As a result, only three reporters declared an interest in being travelling companions for Polo. The other two were 'rookies' and considered worthy of careful nurturing but not experienced enough to take on this particular task. Marcus, on the other foot, was expendable.

What Caxton and his cohorts did not realise, though, was that Marcus was far from stupid. For the hierarchy at the *Standard*, a lack of confidence was seen as a lack of both intelligence and personality. But what the hierarchy had overlooked was that Marcus had had to earn the approval of Polo, who was extremely particular about who he travelled with. Perhaps such a factor would have been borne in mind if there had not been so many other topics to think about.

Yet the reclusive Polo, a mouse with a mystical air about him, knew what he wanted. He did not know how his latest venture would pan out, but first and foremost, he expected loyalty from travelling companions who had no doubts about who was the boss.

Unquestioning gerbils and hamsters could be relied on in these respects.

But what Polo wanted was a variety of qualities that even the bravest and most erudite mice could not offer. He wanted a mouse who could sum up a situation quickly, adapt to it and, if asked, give an accurate assessment of whatever events might follow. His chosen mouse had to be brave, intuitive, sensitive and, if Polo became incapacitated in any way, capable of making independent decisions and, if absolutely necessary, even taking over.

There was no doubt in Polo's mind that Marcus had all these qualities in abundance. An enthusiastic student of mouse nature, with an ability to discretely find things out, he was well aware of how Marcus was looked upon by Caxton and co. And, although he would never admit it, he took delight in confounding the findings of other 'amateur psychologists'.

Polo was equally aware that he and his expedition force would be slipping away almost unnoticed, as all eyes and thoughts were on other matters generally and the 'Mega Mouse and Cat Games' in particular.

The first fans of the Games, due to take place in three days' time, were already beginning to arrive in Phoenix from the smaller towns and villages. The hoteliers and hostel keepers were, as always at this time of year, at full stretch. The Mouse Police, meanwhile, were preparing for the arrival of the Trojans. There had always been intense rivalry between the two towns, and this could often lead to flare-ups, fights and nights spent in cells. Gerbils and hamsters could be seen scurrying around the Big Cheese Sports Stadium with brooms, spades, hosepipes and steamrollers in an effort to ensure that everything inside was pristine.

The hoteliers and hostel keepers began to take in their first arrivals. Much of the accommodation was underground, with access provided by buses, buggies and miniature tube trains. Garages and buggy ports were available, too, and all these facilities were brain children of Da Vinci.

In common with many of the above-ground homes, some hotels were at the tops of sturdy stilts. Many of the underground and overground rooms would have remained empty during the Temperate Season, when the Games and certain other events were not taking place. Now, the demand for them was acute, especially for the rooms on stilts, which could be reached via lifts and offered spectacular views for miles around.

Mobile cheese bars began to appear in the streets. Traffic wardens, displaying renewed airs of self-importance, began to patrol them. Ticket touts and bookies began to appear and made no attempt to conceal their air of shiftiness. Hamsters, gerbils and lower-class mice were beavering away with cleaning materials to ensure that the roads near the stadium were clean and litter kept to a minimum.

Market traders began to stock up their stalls to bulging point, causing consternation among nearby established shopkeepers. Yet, all the traders, indoors and out, had the same mission in mind: to tempt visitors to the Games to leave the stadium for a while and come their way, too.

As the big day drew closer, the Trojans, who had previously been arriving in fits and starts, began to appear in droves. About half of them headed for various types of accommodation, which had been pre-booked. The others brought along tents, caravans, camper vans and other types of vehicles and set up camp around the town's periphery. The Mouse Police patrols were doubled, in anticipation of unruly behaviour. Unprecedented profits seemed to be on the cards every year. So, too, was trouble.

On the day itself, the police presence at and near the Big Cheese Stadium was more apparent than ever. This particularly applied to the queues leading to the turnstile gates and the three roads that led to them.

The stadium itself resembled a giant, dome-shaped piece of Edam, wrapped in red. It was open-topped, however, and this fact became apparent to customers once they were inside. On top of the highest hill in town, surrounded by the widest of moats and built on a mouse-made mound to make it safe from the worst possible floods, it could be seen from miles away from all directions. To walk round the stadium, after crossing one of the moat bridges, took at least ten minutes. Visitors to the small gates that led to the turnstiles were greeted by assiduous cashiers, some of them gerbils and hamsters. The police ensured that the queues were orderly.

The stadium seats, which were collapsible and tended to clatter in unison whenever audience members chose to stand en masse to applaud a memorable moment – or simply to perform a 'Mexican wave' – were accessed by long, covered corridors. As customers reached the end of any one of the corridors, they could not fail to be awestruck… however many times they had been to the stadium before.

The Big Cheese Stadium was widely regarded as the island's pièce de résistance. Big enough to accommodate several football pitches, it catered for every activity imaginable. Football and rugby fixtures, athletics meetings, tennis, squash and badminton tournaments, boxing, bowls, dancing, films, plays, operas, concerts and stage shows were all regular events. All were well attended, and none less so than the annual Mouse and Cat Games. Much of the inside was laid to lawn, much of it immaculately manicured. Some was under asphalt or concrete, and various mouse-made structures were on hand to provide cover or otherwise enhance facilities when needed.

Restaurants, cafes, pubs, and milk and cheese bars could be found at ground-floor level or on some of the tiers that lined the stadium walls and supported seating. Some of the seats were at ground-floor level, though most were ranged around the sides on row after row. For spectators occupying the rows at or near the top, the animals taking part in the events below resembled tiny dots, while the circular space that looked up at the sky made the spectators feel tiny, too.

As always, the events were heralded by a twenty-strong band, whose members marched robustly around the periphery and then towards a podium that had been set up in the centre. The music the band played was robust, too, and gave an impression of military might. As the band reached the podium, a troupe of dancing female hamsters in rah-rah skirts appeared from one of the entrance corridors and treated the audience to a display of high kicking and swivelling hips. Then, as the dancers sauntered off, a group of gymnasts appeared and put on a display of agility and muscularity. Highlights included vaulting over a wooden horse, tumbling through hoops and various feats of strength by Adonis. As always, the mighty Sports Editor was able to draw applause as he did press-ups with two gerbils sitting on his back and then raised aloft a five hundred-pound hunk of cheese.

Next on the agenda was hare racing, an event which saw a toy greyhound propelled round a circular track before six lean and muscular bucks sprang from traps and vied to be first to catch their quarry. Speculation on which hare would win lasted longer than the race itself and usually turned out to be a money-spinner for the bookies, who were amazingly adept at working out the odds and rarely got it wrong. On this occasion, however, and against all the odds, the winner turned out to be Bionic Tortoise, a two hundred-to-one outsider. The outcome meant rich pickings for a few punters, who had fancied a wild flutter, and a disaster for the 'experts'.

Perhaps it was just as well, that light relief came in the form of dogs being chased round an arena by cats. The canines varied considerably in size, ranging from the diminutive mastiff to the bulky dachshund. But their animosity towards cats, displayed with spitting and arched backs, was uniform. The outcomes of the chases were more or less the same, too, with the cats becoming increasingly frustrated as their natural enemies disappeared through holes or jumped on top of various boxes that had been specially laid out for the occasion. Each individual outcome was the subject of much mirth among the spectators, who, as rodents, hated all felines.

Mirth gave way to bloodlust when it was time for the main event to get underway. The cat was unquestionably the number-one hate figure for all but the most eccentric rodents. Several minutes elapsed between the end of the dog chases and the moment every member of the audience had been waiting for. Before a baying crowd, the band played a medley of music that reflected the mood of hatred, violence, expectation and revenge. The reason for the latter was unclear, though every mouse present was gripped with a primeval urge to eradicate some form of horror that had prevailed in a bygone age and see the maximum retribution exacted.

First to emerge from the corridors were the objects of hate. They appeared from every direction and came in every shape and form and both genders. Only the kittens were spared, along with the two most fertile mothers because the need to breed future performers was always borne in mind. Black cats, white cats, black and white cats, tabby cats, tortoiseshell cats and grey cats all entered the arena to the sound of ironic cheers. The only feline to receive anything remotely resembling an accolade was an elderly ginger tom with matted fur, battered features and scars that served as evidence of many a past battle. The tom had somehow survived three previous Mouse and Cat Games and now was the subject of grudging respect… even to the extent of being known as 'The Tom'.

The cheering and jeering went on for several minutes as the ill-fated felines scuttled this way and that in fruitless searches for means of escaping or simply assumed positions of abject surrender.

The appearance of their executioners was heralded with a strident fanfare. Ten muscular mice, most of them ginger mice, made their entrance to the most rapturous cheers yet. All ten wore chain mail as protection against claws and teeth and all ten carried swords and shields. In practice, the chain mail and shields were rarely needed as the cats' weapons of destruction had been blunted in advance, and the swords were often jettisoned after the initial chase had rendered the quarry beaten before the 'battle'. As expected, only 'The Tom' displayed any real signs of defiance.

The 'battle' – or, to be precise, slaughter – began after the blowing of a whistle. The captive cats ran frantically but quickly discovered that there was nowhere to hide. The warrior mice were conscious that they could win prizes, awarded by a panel of judges for the most kills, the most spectacular kill and the most entertaining one. They did their best to make the carnage something to behold.

A popular ploy was to toy with the cats by trapping them, pinning them to the ground and then letting them go for a moment or two before trapping them again. Some felines fell for this ploy five or six times before being crushed and devoured. Some of the mouse warriors were adept at repeatedly knocking a cat several feet into the air before administering the same fate. And, as all this took place, the onlooking rodents were increasingly worked up into a frenzy.

Perhaps inevitably, the denouement was the demise of 'The Tom'. The battle-scarred arch enemy of all rodents was up against the might of Adonis. Outweighed and over-matched, 'The Tom' growled, bared his teeth, lunged and lashed out with long, exposed claws – that had not been blunted – but to no avail, before giving up and exposing his ageing body in an act of surrender. Adonis, who had gained the ascendancy almost immediately, took a few steps to one side where he had left his heaviest sword, picked it up and delivered the coup de grâce. In so doing, he brought an end to a Games that many predicted would become the most memorable.

CHAPTER 4

As always, the outcomes of the Mouse and Cat Games were the main topics of conversation for several days afterwards in Phoenix and, to a slightly lesser extent, elsewhere. Before long, however, the attention of the populace began to switch to the forthcoming elections. Early indications were that they would be keenly contested and potentially steeped in controversy.

As a consequence, the news that Polo was about to embark on his most hazardous outing yet almost went unnoticed. The self-effacing Marcus, who, paradoxically, craved attention and recognition, was relieved about this, as he could prepare for his opportunity to shock his detractors with a feat of derring-do that would shake the Isle of Andronicus to its core.

While the Mouse and Cat Games were taking place, he had received a surprise visit at the *Standard* by Polo, who had interviewed him briefly – not the other way round – and left, secure in the knowledge that he had picked the right mouse for the job. At the time, Marcus was unaware that the great explorer had asked a lot of questions to a lot of mice in advance.

Inevitably, there was some interest in an expedition of such magnitude in the newsroom… though far less than there would have been in different circumstances.

However, there were two colleagues who showed more than a passing interest. One was Phaedra, the flirtatious Features Editor, who was to collaborate with Marcus in producing a series of reports and articles relating to the expedition. The other was the veteran Feature Writer, Cicero, who wanted to know not only more about the island but also everything he could about how its population evolved.

Phaedra was the first to buttonhole Marcus, as the latter sat at his desk contemplating what might lie ahead of him. She emerged from her small but pucker office – which was situated a few feet away from Caxton's much bigger one – flounced towards where he sat, found a seat for herself and placed herself well within touching distance. She gazed into Marcus's eyes with the sort of intensity that was usually reserved only for Adonis.

"So, you're all set to go, then!" Phaedra said, as Marcus fidgeted. "Are you having second thoughts?"

"Not at all," Marcus replied unconvincingly.

"Good for you!" Phaedra exclaimed. "You must be apprehensive, though?"

"Just a little bit!"

Phaedra eyed Marcus speculatively for a moment before asking: "What made you want to go on this expedition in the first place?" Then, before Marcus could answer, she added: "You have always seemed a bit of a timid type to me… no offense, of course!"

"None taken," Marcus replied, both warily and wearily. The observation was not welcome, but Phaedra's personality enabled her to get away with it. "I would like to know more about the island," he offered.

"Is that it… nothing else?"

"Not quite. I have never really done anything exciting in my life and, I suppose, like many others, find that I want to have one great adventure. I want something that I can look back on with fondness and pride and perhaps tell my story to the next generation."

Phaedra's eyes lit up. "You don't have any offspring, do you?" she observed. "At least, not as far as we know."

An embarrassed Marcus could not look her in the eye. "No, I'm not married," he mumbled. "You never know what's round the corner, though!"

Phaedra then decided to change tack. After asking Marcus what he knew about Polo, and being told 'not much', she focused on the expedition itself. "Who's going with you? And for how long?" Then, after writing down what she felt was a semblance of an itinerary, she wished Marcus the best of luck and said she would see him later.

Listening from his usual corner was Cicero, whose hearing was acute despite his advancing years. The veteran Feature Writer was renowned in equal measure for his talent, individuality, eccentricity and occasional awkwardness. No other mouse at the *Standard* could turn a phrase or, when the situation demanded, wax lyrical in the way that only he could. His intellect was hard to match, too, and it was only an innate rebellious streak that kept him from climbing the career ladder. And, in fact, the very word 'promotion' was anathema to him.

On top of all this, Cicero had a reputation for the numbers of bees he had in his bonnet. Bullies and creeps, in particular, had reason to fear him.

The biggest bee by far, though, was Cicero's obsession with the 'Origins of Mousekind'. He refused to accept that life began and ended on the Isle of Andronicus. He insisted that there was life elsewhere, quite possibly a different form of life. And, above all, he refused to believe that mice were always the dominant beings. He wanted to know why mice, gerbils, hamsters and other rodents walked on two legs, while other mammals walked on four. Although unable to provide evidence, he was convinced that mice were once subservient to other beings and were now only top of the tree because of some yet-to-be-determined freak of nature or some other influence.

In different circumstances, Cicero would have moved heaven and earth to be part of Polo's expedition. He had met Polo and talked to him at length about his pet subject and received a sympathetic hearing. But his age and state of health, that included respiratory problems, put paid to any such hope. Whether Polo would have accepted a younger, healthier Cicero was questionable, in any case. Polo expected those who joined him to accept that whatever he said went, and it was by no means certain that Cicero would have complied.

The fact that Polo had accepted Marcus for such a role had initially made him intensely jealous. However, jealousy quickly gave way to the realisation that he and Marcus could be something approaching kindred spirits, even allies.

"When do you set off?" he asked once Phaedra had gone.

"In the next day or so," Marcus replied. "We've got a long way to go, and we need to be back before the season ends, of course."

"You know I'm as jealous as hell, don't you?!" Cicero said with a rueful smile.

Marcus apologised and promised to give him a full account on returning.

"I'd appreciate that," said Cicero. "As you know, I'm always banging on about where we really came from, and if you can find anything about that – anything at all – I would be really interested. Come to think of it, there's no end of stuff to be found out, and I have a feeling you might be the one to crack it."

Cicero's words rang into Marcus's ears for hours afterwards. So, too, unfortunately, did Phaedra's. Was he the right rodent to crack the conundrum concerning mousekind's origins, let alone justify his place on Polo's expedition? Or was he, as Phaedra had suggested, too timid? The questions came up in his mind again and again, and the answers kept changing! What Marcus was clear about, though, was that he was tired of being seen as timid. He wanted the entire population of Andronicus to see him as anything but!

He looked back on a puphood that was blighted by shyness. There was nothing wrong with his pedigree, but he lacked self-esteem. Prior to puberty, he was small for his age, unprepossessing and hardly ever able to please his cantankerous parents. His father was a renowned academic from respectable but moderate mouse stock, while his mother was unquestionably upper class and famed in the highest social circles for her beauty.

Marcus Senior was born in Carthage. On the death of his father, a humble clerk at a grain market, he moved with his mother at an early age to Troy. His academic ability soon became apparent, and his mother began to live her life through him and ensured that he had the best possible private education. He excelled in every subject and was highly competent at sports as well. His main forte, though, was maths and, as an adult, he became a leading educationist, businessmouse and politician... rubbing shoulders with the likes of Da Vinci, the Prime Minister of the day and a young Polo.

Marcus's mother, Cleopatra, a native of Troy, was of the highest pedigree possible and regarded as the perfect catch for a well-heeled bachelor. However, her intellect came nowhere near to matching her lineage and, just beneath the surface and unknown to all but a few, there were serious mental health issues.

Marcus Senior had high expectations of Marcus Junior and became increasingly frustrated by his son's inability to come even close to matching his own exacting standards. His frustrations were fuelled by the actions of his wayward wife, whose only interest in Marcus Junior was instilling social skills of the highest order and who spent much of her time mixing in circles in which breeding transcended intellect. Domestic rows became commonplace, each parent had a string of affairs and Cleopatra had two nervous breakdowns before committing suicide.

Almost immediately after his mother died, Marcus Junior was packed off to a boarding school in Phoenix.

The Cheese and Wheat School for Young Male Mice was the most prestigious educational establishment of them all. Its fees were sky high, but there was no shortage of parents in the upper echelons of society who were prepared to pay. The parents were secure in the knowledge that time spent at the 'Cheese and Wheat' nearly always led to a university place or, failing that, a choice but undemanding job found through the 'Old Mouse Network'. Strong emphasis was placed on sport, too, and Adonis, with his massive strength, was among those who flourished.

Places at the 'Cheese and Wheat' were limited, though, with a maximum of sixteen per class and just two classes for each year. Nearly all the places went to those who lived in or just outside Phoenix and, before Marcus's arrival, none to a Trojan. Only exceptional circumstances allowed Marcus to be granted entry. One factor was that any link with a father who had achieved so much in so many fields of endeavour would mean even more prestige for the school. Another was an offer by Marcus Senior to act as patron and benefactor for some of the school's projects. Yet another was a willingness to pay more than the going rate, even though the school's fees were considered to be inflated already. Eventually, the school head caved in under the relentless pressure Marcus Senior had put him under and agreed to admit his son… even though he was a Trojan.

Newcomers tended to receive a lively reception at the 'Cheese and Wheat'. At the very least, they were the butt of a variety of practical jokes. Some of the jokes were innocuous and easy to laugh off, while others could border on sadistic. The question of what types of joke a 'newbie' would be subjected to depended largely on his behaviour and how he reacted initially. Many of the young mice, as natives of Phoenix, knew each other already. They had a fair inkling of what to expect and regarded initiation as a form of camaraderie.

Marcus, who had no idea of what to expect at all, soon became the target for special treatment. Once it became known that he was an 'alien' from Troy, the other 'newbies' were largely ignored. Some of them joined forces with the established pupils, largely as a means of self-preservation, and helped them to administer various forms of torment. These ranged from unremitting teasing to pushing Marcus's head into a lavatory bowl, covering him with excrement and pulling the chain. Unwanted objects would frequently be found in Marcus's desk, satchel and bed. Books or items of sports kit would go missing at critical times, and Marcus would be tripped up 'accidentally on purpose' almost every day.

At the end of the first term, there was no going back to Troy. Marcus's father had told the school he had both a mountain of work and health issues to deal with and would therefore be unable to look after him. So, the young Marcus stayed behind with a handful of other pupils, none of them in the same year as him, though a number did turn up in the daytime to attend holiday classes. Makeshift meals were served from trolleys, a library was left open for pupils wishing to study independently and at night, Marcus slept alone in a dormitory while a janitor assumed charge of the entire school premises.

The second term heralded the arrival of, among others, Toby, who came from inferior mouse stock but possessed exceptional scholastic qualifications. He was even smaller and slighter than Marcus, was untidy in his ways, unkempt in appearance and had the unfortunate habit of scratching his bottom while speaking. As a result, a lot of the attention previously reserved for Marcus now focused on Toby. Marcus and Toby sought solace in each other's company, while all their contemporaries labelled them 'the misfits'. Eventually, the teasing and bullying abated, due to boredom among the tormentors, and 'the misfits' were sent to Coventry instead.

"I wonder where the term 'sent to Coventry' came from," Toby said to Marcus ruefully.

At the end of the second term, Toby was able to go back home to be with his parents, while Marcus had to stay put. To all intents and purposes, he was on his own again, and more and more, he took to frequenting the library. Here was a place where he could hone his slowly emerging skills as a writer. His ability to accurately and descriptively report events as they occurred, and also produce creative and imaginative fiction, would, in time, become his path to something approaching social acceptance. When not writing, he would love to read the works, fictional and otherwise, of established authors. These would include scientific manuals by Da Vinci, tales of discovery by Polo and adventure yarns by Caxton. Perhaps the most absorbing material of all, however, came from Cicero, a former pupil, who had penned his first thesis on the 'Origins of Mousekind'.

Life became a little easier for the two 'misfits' during the third and final term of the school year. Their scholastic achievements earned praise from teachers and grudging respect from their contemporaries. Toby's all-round academic status prompted some to seek his help and guidance with projects they found challenging. Toby was well aware of the power this gave him, and he ceased to be bullied. Marcus, meanwhile, was able to enthral with the stories he wrote and which were frequently read out by one of the teachers.

Marcus was beginning to grow rapidly, too, and, at the same time, gaining recognition as a promising boxer. New clothes needed to be ordered for him in a hurry and, before the term ended, he was well on his way to becoming a tall, strong and well-groomed young rodent with looks that could turn female heads. Unfortunately, though, he was too diffident and lacking in confidence to fully appreciate the transformation.

The end of the third term heralded the end of the first academic year. Marcus was at last able to return to Troy, ostensibly to be with his father. The break, sadly, turned out to be a lonely one, with Marcus Senior having to pay frequent hospital visits and, in any case, having little time for his son. The young Trojan mice, with their animosity towards anything remotely connected with Phoenix, would have nothing to do with Marcus Junior at all.

Life as a second-year pupil at the 'Cheese and Wheat' was a significant improvement, especially after ten weeks of being ostracised, and Marcus even began to enjoy it there. Then, disaster struck. His father died of a respiratory infection, and the money to cover school fees dried up. So, at the end of the first term of the second year, Marcus had to say farewell to Toby and a few other newly found friends and return to Troy.

He went to live with an aunt, who sent him to a local school with a vastly inferior reputation. His fellow pupils were, by and large, the ones who had been ostracising him because of his link with Phoenix, and he became a social outcast once more.

CHAPTER 5

Marcus made sure for the last time that he had not forgotten to pack anything. His buggy awaited and he climbed in and started to drive without looking back. There was no looking back now. He had committed himself to an adventure so extreme that not even Polo had much idea of what might transpire during the course of it.

The road ahead was straight, smooth and flat for just over fifty miles before Marcus turned right into a road that was hilly, bumpy and potholed. Phoenix could be seen no longer, and Marcus was heading northwards towards where the reclusive Polo lived and used as a starting point for most of his expeditions.

Polo's home was a cave halfway up a steep hill that lay almost exactly equidistant between Phoenix and Troy, the island's two main towns. The cave was accessed via a narrow, winding path. Marcus parked his buggy in a hut-cum-garage that lay on a flat area just below where the path started. The structure – which could, at a pinch, be inhabited – and its surrounds had been created by Polo, with a little help from Da Vinci. The beginning of the path was half hidden by bushes and grasses, and Marcus had to consult written directions he had received in advance to locate it. Having done so, he clambered up a small grass bank and passed between two prickly bushes to reach it.

The path was steep, stony and stamina-sapping, and it took Marcus a good hour to reach the cave entrance. "He must have done this on purpose!" he muttered to himself as he huffed and puffed his way to the cave... unaware that Polo liked to test his fellow mice at every opportunity, especially the ones he did not know so well.

Eventually, the mouth came into view, as did a grinning Polo. "Welcome to my lair!" he said, with more than a hint of a gloat. "Come in and make yourself at home."

An exhausted Marcus half tripped over the baggage he had hauled up the path as he entered. The baggage included clothing to cater for all weathers, plus a number of travelling aids that might or might not be needed. As Polo had emphasised at the outset, most of the journey would be into the unknown.

"My part-time housekeeper Quickly will take you to your room," Polo said in a tone of utmost authority. The legendary explorer was no more than five foot six even when standing up straight – which was not often – but he possessed a presence that was unfailingly dominating. The reason, perhaps, was a pair of piercing blue eyes that seemed to bore their way through any mouse he might be talking to and, at other times, seek out hidden horizons.

Quickly – a compliant, comely and diminutive gerbil – motioned Marcus to follow and took him to a room at the back. Marcus could not fail to notice that the cave was compact, kept in apple-pie order and seemed to contain no more than the bare necessities.

"Please make yourself comfortable," Quickly said to him as he entered a bedroom that was small but offered such creature comforts as an en-suite shower room, tea-making facilities, a television and a selection of pillows. "Supper will be in half an hour."

Marcus slumped into an armchair that lay a couple of feet from the bed, and the next thing he knew, Quickly was shaking him by a shoulder and telling him it was time to eat. Quickly led him to a room that was only slightly bigger than his bedroom but contained all of Polo's best furniture, including a mahogany dining table and matching chairs. Marcus knew immediately that he was in a room reserved for special occasions only.

"Sit down and make yourself comfortable," said Polo, who was seated at the head of the table already. He instructed Marcus to sit to his right. Three of the other chairs were occupied by Quickly and the other travellers.

"Let me introduce you to Rosencrantz and Boxer, who will be with us on our venture tomorrow," Polo added. "Rosencrantz is a dab hand at just about everything – be it cooking, mending, finding his way around or getting out of tricky situations – while Boxer has muscles. Rosencrantz can concoct a meal out of almost anything and repair a radio that anyone else would deem irreparable, while Boxer can carry heavy baggage forever and, if necessary, move massive obstacles."

Rosencrantz was a gerbil and a cousin of Quickly. He was of similar size to Polo and shared his wiriness, too. Boxer, a hamster, was almost as big as Adonis, but possessed none of the *Standard* Sports Editor's intellect or vanity.

Quickly disappeared and returned to serve the first course, which was cat's fur soup with wheat grain. The soup, which was highly popular as an hors d'oeuvre, contained only faint traces of fur but included all the nutrients that had lain embedded in it and had not been washed away by a feline tongue. The grain that floated on top combined well with these nutrients to create a much-sought-after tangy flavour. The main course was, inevitably, cheese. However, the cheese, served hot, cold and on various plates, was of the highest quality and had been carefully stored and cooked to perfection. The diners squeaked with satisfaction at regular intervals during this course, and then again once this course was finished and Quickly produced bowls of berries and bottles of the best wine.

The diners hardly talked at all as they enjoyed their meal, and Polo refrained from mentioning what lay ahead the next day. As it happened, Rosencrantz, Boxer and even Marcus had little knowledge or interest in wine, though Quickly made a brief attempt to start a discussion on how it became popular in the first place. "Perhaps this is something we should ask Da Vinci," she eventually said.

"Or Cicero," Marcus added. "With his various attempts to find out where we all came from, perhaps he will, one day, be able to say where we came from!"

The tyro explorer's tongue-in-cheek quip led to nervous laughter, followed by silence. Every rodent at the table had been reminded with a jolt what they were there for. Quickly took this moment as a cue to clear the table and withdraw.

Polo was on cue, too. "I very much hope you enjoyed your meal," he said, rising onto his hindfeet. "Have a good night's sleep… the work starts tomorrow."

CHAPTER 6

News of Polo's latest venture had reached Carthage, a town that tended to receive news late, when Polo and his party arrived there. The travellers were treated royally. A sumptuous meal was laid on in the town hall, with music, dancing and speeches galore by local dignitaries. Even Rosencrantz and Boxer were accorded a level of respect that was usually reserved for upper-class mice only. Every rodent in town wanted to meet the quartet, who were also offered accommodation at the most prestigious hotel. The night of luxury was the last the four adventurers could expect to enjoy for a long time.

The following morning, they were back on the road and following a route that continued for four hundred miles along the west coast, before turning sharply to the right just under twenty miles from the edge of The Oven. What lay beyond was a matter of speculation. Villagers and farm workers waved and wished them good luck from the roadside as they went. The numbers of well-wishers slowly thinned out, however, and were non-existent for the next thirty miles.

All of a sudden, the road came to an end. From now on, the party had to rely on nature-made tracks and terrain that would, hopefully, be passable. The character of the landscape began to change subtly and the sky assumed an air of brooding menace. A gentle breeze gave way to a chill wind that almost reached gale force.

Big black rocks – some rounded, some craggy – came into view as the buggy traversed along what passed for a path. The sky changed colour at regular intervals, as if reacting to a succession of challenges being thrown at it by nature. It could be scarlet at one moment and azure blue at another, before turning grey, black, dappled and even rainbow-ridden. For much of the time it gave the impression that it was closing in on the quartet and about to envelope them. Even Polo had never seen anything quite like it.

Driving the buggy became increasingly hard work as it travelled upwards and downwards on an undulating track and coped with rocks, stones, mud, sand, slippery grass and even mini quagmires. Boxer relieved Rosencrantz at the wheel, and Polo and Marcus were obliged to take turns, too. Yet, as they battled with the elements, the four travellers all experienced a feeling of exhilaration that transcended apprehension. The pioneering spirit had taken over, and even Marcus was able to believe he was one of the mightiest of mice.

The quartet were, after all, entering the unknown, where, at least as far as they knew, no other rodent had dared to tread. They did not know what lay ahead or what they would find. And they were not entirely sure why they were there, anyway...

The undulations gradually became sharper and steeper and, after about half an hour, the buggy reached a plateau that seemed to stretch endlessly ahead, and on the left and right as well. The temperature dipped to just above freezing and the whole area was gripped by a wind that had nothing to halt it and made the temperature seem much lower than it actually was. Polo and his party were all glad to have brought along extra layers of clothing.

There was now no track to speak of, but the buggy, with its outsize wheels and tyres, was well able to cope with the lumps, bumps, holes and sharp stones that might well have disabled a vehicle that had not been specially customised.

However, signs of life were non-existent, save blades of grass that rose no more than fingernail height, and this was disconcerting. There were no birds, no trees, no flowers or other plants, not even an ant or a fly.

Eventually, and without warning, night fell. The darkness descended so quickly that the buggy, driven at the time by Marcus, had to come to a halt. The four travellers remained where they were and slept as well as they could. Six hours later, dawn broke with similar suddenness. The trek continued and the terrain did not alter for the entire day. Nightfall arrived abruptly again, but this time the travellers were forewarned, and under Polo's direction, they were able to erect two tents for sleeping in and also prepare an evening meal, plus breakfast for the following morning.

Another day and a half passed before there was any sign of a change. The plateau, at last, began to slope upwards at an increasingly sharp angle. A white cloud floated just above the horizon and, as the buggy climbed, it did not seem to change its position. After a time, the buggy passed under it and then, it seemed, through it. The wind and temperature both dropped, and visibility became almost non-existent.

The travellers could only guess what lay ahead, though they were thankful that their mode of transport had got them as far as it did. When darkness showed signs of descending once more, Polo said it was time to set up camp, eat, sleep… and try not to contemplate too much on what lay in store for the quartet until the morning.

Not surprisingly, all four were awake and prepared to move on long before the sun began to show itself. They had slept fitfully, to say the least. As the sun started to rise and try to make its presence felt, the way ahead was obscured by both the cloud and a grey, murky mist that seemed to come from nowhere. So, after a hurried breakfast, it was back to the buggy with feelings of both expectation and apprehension.

The gradient continued to sharpen and there were more obstacles in the forms of boulders that tended to remain unseen until just a foot away. The buggy was now being put to the test, and the matter of how long travel in it could continue became open to conjecture.

"It can only be a matter of time before we're going to have to walk," Marcus said nervously.

"Don't be such a pessimist!" the redoubtable Boxer retorted.

"I think Marcus is probably right," said Rosencrantz. "However, what will be will be. There's no turning back, that's for sure!"

Polo gave a nod of approval. "I'm glad you said that!" he added with a wry smile.

Polo, whose turn it was to drive at the time, suddenly gave a start and slammed on the brakes as, without warning, a massive bank of stones loomed just inches away. The quartet looked upwards to observe that beyond the stone bank was a cliff or mountain that was sheer, dark grey in hue and seemed to go upwards forever. The cloud thinned for a moment, and the travellers could see that the cliff or mountain was as wide as it was high – perhaps wider – and that there was no way for them to go except straight ahead. Marcus, Rosencrantz and Boxer each looked at Polo and could see from his facial expression that the idea of going back should not even be mentioned.

The bank of stones was about eight feet high. There was nothing for it but to leave the buggy where it was and pack rucksacks with as many provisions as possible before clambering over the stones and, after that, ascending whatever lay beyond. Without Boxer, getting over the stone bank would have been extremely difficult. But, in the event, the mighty hamster was able to help the other three over with a bit of lifting and pushing from behind before hurling over the bulging rucksacks and half vaulting, half climbing himself.

Once over, the four felt they had entered a different world. The only view from the back was the wall they had just climbed. Almost immediately to the front was a sheer rock face that disappeared into the sky and seemed to go on forever, vertically and laterally. Making an ascent appeared to be impossible.

"What in heaven do we do now?" Marcus asked Polo.

Polo looked to the left, right and upwards before replying, "I don't know. All I do know is that there is no going back." The others nodded nervously.

"There must be a way up somewhere," Rosencrantz said with as much conviction as he could muster.

"We will just have to look until we find it," Marcus said with renewed courage.

Polo pulled out two whistles from a zipped front pocket and handed one of them to Marcus. "OK, you and Rosencrantz can look to the left, and Boxer and I will go right," he said. "If you find anything, blow your whistle at full blast and we'll be coming running! We will do the same, of course."

The search in either direction entailed looking upwards and, at the same time, downwards to avoid stumbling on one of the many stones and rocks that impeded progress on a narrow, undulating path. Eventually, the eagle-eyed Rosencrantz spotted what looked like a narrow, winding path about forty feet up. It appeared to have been carved out of a small indentation in the rock face. There was no way of telling from ground level how long the path was – assuming it was a path – let alone where it might lead them. However, the search had been going on for a good hour, and the discovery seemed to offer the only glimmer of hope. So, Marcus blew the whistle he had been issued with and, to his surprise, created a sound that could be heard miles away.

Polo and Boxer appeared and told the other two that their equally arduous search had been fruitless. Polo eyed his three companions for a few moments, before saying in the challenging tone he was known for: "We all knew it wasn't going to be easy, didn't we?" He gazed again at the others, and Marcus in particular, before adding: "We have no other option… now let's get on with it!"

"What if the path isn't a path or if it leads to nowhere?" protested Marcus.

"Perhaps just one of us should go up and have a recce first?" a placatory Rosencrantz suggested.

"Marcus does have a point," Boxer added.

Polo saw that this was the time to show the others that he was not just their leader but a leader who would not expect anyone to undertake a task he could not handle himself. "Fair enough!" he said. "You can all wait here while I go and have a look."

Without further ado, the great explorer clambered upwards. Although well into middle age, he demonstrated a level of agility that many a younger rodent would envy, and it seemed to be no time at all before he reached what looked like a path. He then disappeared.

Marcus, Rosencrantz and Boxer waited anxiously down below. And they waited and waited! Marcus and Boxer became particularly concerned, but Rosencrantz, who was the most aware of his leader's capabilities, persuaded the others to trust him and just wait. "He's gone off on his own many a time before and he knows what he's doing," the gerbil said. So, when nightfall arrived and there was still no sign of Polo, the trio had fewer qualms than they might have had about bedding down until the morning.

Daybreak arrived and breakfast was consumed in silence as three pairs of eyes remained fixed on the path – and it clearly had to be a path – above them and the area around it. Marcus began to show signs of fretting, and Rosencrantz, managing to conceal his own concerns, gave him a reassuring pat on the shoulder. Mid-morning began to beckon. As it did, Boxer pointed towards the path to indicate that Polo had come into view. The celebrated explorer again displayed agility that belied his age as he descended. "What's for breakfast?" he asked, as he reached the others.

Marcus had a rummage in his rucksack, produced a hunk of cheese and asked, tongue in cheek: "What kept you?!"

Polo grabbed the cheese almost rudely and, a bite and a munch later, retorted: "You are about to find out!" The others realised there was no point in asking anything else before their leader was fed and ready to answer. They could see he was weary as well. After finishing his snack, Polo announced that he needed to 'chill for a bit'. He spotted a piece of ground that was comparatively soft, found a blanket, got under it and went straight to sleep.

"He will be awake in a couple of hours and be as bright as a button," Rosencrantz said. "He doesn't need the same amount of sleep as the rest of us."

The prediction was spot on. After exactly two hours, Polo surfaced, packed away the blanket he had slept under and made his long-awaited announcement: "The path is going to lead us to new discoveries. I can feel it in my bones. I don't know exactly what it will lead us to, but I know that we absolutely must take it. I have a nose for this sort of thing, and my nose never lets me down."

"How long is the path?" Marcus asked.

"It went on for miles and, at one point, I thought it was going to go on forever. I even thought of giving up and going back."

"Is there something to see at the end?" Rosencrantz interjected.

"Oh, yes! After what seemed like an eternity, I suddenly came out of the side of a mountain and was dazzled by what lay ahead. I had come out into a massive new area, a sort of plateau, that had mountains on all sides. One of the mountains seemed to glisten with gold – though, I'm not sure about this – and at that stage, I decided to turn back and collect you lot."

The other three gazed at where Polo had come from. "How do we get up there?" Marcus asked. "I, for one, am not so agile as you."

Polo produced a hammer and chisel and promised to create footholds. A few minutes later, he was doing exactly that. Rosencrantz, who was almost as nimble as his leader, followed and coaxed Marcus, who climbed behind Polo, into using the holes and not looking down. Boxer, who, as always, carried the lion's share of the baggage, took up the rear. In doing so, he was well placed to rescue Marcus if the expedition reporter should slip. That was not necessary, however, as slowly but surely, all four made it to the path.

Polo could see that Marcus had grown grey at the gills and was breathing heavily. So, with a directive driven by expediency as much as compassion, he said: "Let's give ourselves a moment or two before we move on."

After ten minutes, Polo began to follow the path to the left and motioned the others to go with him. The path was narrow, and the quartet had to walk in single file. At first, they were out in the open with a sheer drop to one side and a mountainside that seemed to rise forever above them on the other. Before long, however, the travellers were in a tunnel. Boxer, who was still at the rear, handed out torches and the trek continued. The path remained narrow and walls either side allowed no room for deviation. Headroom was limited at times, and it was often necessary to stoop. On one occasion, the path dipped alarmingly and then went upwards at a gradient of one in four. The journey through the tunnel went on for hours and seemed interminable.

Yet the experience was less claustrophobic than it might have been, and the air quality was better than Polo feared it would be. There were times when the air was musty, while at other times it was dank, and for about twenty minutes, it smelled of rotting meat. Yet, dominating the air at all times was a chill wind that forced the travellers to don extra layers of clothing but, at the same time, allowed breathing to be reasonably comfortable.

"We must be in the bowels of some massive mountain," Marcus observed. "It's really exciting... though I hope it won't be much longer before we're in the open again."

"Me, too," agreed Boxer. "I've never known anything like this."

"Me neither," said Rosencrantz, who, with the other two, waited to hear whether Polo had anything to say.

Their leader obliged. "I've never known anything quite like this either. And I don't just mean this tunnel. I mean the expedition as a whole... so far," he said.

"So, what do you reckon lies ahead?" Marcus asked.

Polo paused for a moment before replying: "I'm not sure exactly, but my nose tells me we are not far from the end of this tunnel. And, what's more, I believe we are on the verge of making some major discoveries. I also have a feeling that untold riches lie ahead... and, as I have said before, my nose rarely lets me down."

Almost as soon as he had finished speaking, the path widened and rose steeply. After a while, the sound of running water could be heard. The tunnel began to turn into a cavern and, a couple of hundred yards later, the travellers came upon a brook that ran thirty feet below them and could be crossed over by an old, stone bridge. Beyond the brook lay an upwards earthen path, upon which a rivulet of light shone down from an, as yet unseen, hole.

Once over the bridge, Marcus expressed interest in how such a structure, however small, came to be there. "That's not a product of nature. It must have been mouse-made," he suggested.

"A very interesting thought!" Polo agreed. "Perhaps we'll have some answers once we've got through the opening at the end of this path."

The opening turned out to be little more than a small hole, and for Boxer, it was quite a struggle to get through it.

A stunning sight awaited the quartet on the other side.

CHAPTER 7

"What do you mean they're off the air?!" Caxton bellowed. "How can that be possible?!" The Editor's anger could be heard well beyond the walls of his office.

"I'm afraid we haven't been able to make contact for over an hour," Titus told him. "As you know, the lines have been constantly open, and we have been in touch regularly… until now." The Chief Reporter waited nervously for another explosive response.

Caxton calmed down a bit, stroked his chin and said: "Get the engineer to have a look at the radio equipment we have at our end. I've got to go out now. As you know, I have a meeting with the PM."

"I will deal with it," said Titus, not really knowing what the engineer could do to put things right. "I will make sure a reporter is always on hand if we make contact."

"*If* we make contact?! You mean *when*, don't you?!"

Caxton had turned up the volume again and Titus had gone pale. "Leave it with me," the latter murmured. "I hope the meeting goes smoothly, for all our sakes!" he said to himself.

Caxton threw on the top half of his best suit, stormed out of his office, passed the front reception desk and headed towards his designated parking space.

Titus watched him drive off before returning to the newsroom. "Did you hear any of that?" he asked the reporters who were present and not out on assignments.

"It was difficult not to!" said a cynical Cicero.

"So, we've lost touch with Marcus and his expedition, even though Polo's sidekick is a dab hand at fixing broken radios?" the youngest reporter blurted.

"We should get Da Vinci to come up with some more up-to-date equipment," a second reporter commented unhelpfully.

"He doesn't seem to have been around lately," another said. "Rumour has it that he's been busy working on a Flying Machine. Imagine that! Imagine being able to go up in the air and observe everything that goes on down below!"

A harassed Titus began to lose patience. "Look!" he said testily. "We have got a problem, and it needs to be sorted out urgently." He instructed the youngest reporter to contact the firm's engineer post-haste. "And you can all keep on the alert… and let me know as soon as you have got hold of Marcus."

Titus then left the newsroom to see Iago, the Deputy Editor, to discuss what had occurred, as well as how the *Standard* should deal with the run-up to the elections.

Phaedra flounced in, closely followed by Adonis, eager to find out what had caused the rumpus.

Gertrude tried to put them in the picture. "We have lost radio contact with Polo and Marcus, and Caxton's doing his nut!" she said with a wry smile. "He has just stormed out of the building!"

Phaedra smirked. "Interesting!" she observed. "It looks more and more is if His Nibs is so determined to keep the PM sweet that he can't stand the thought of anything possibly spoiling that."

"Do you think there's any truth that Aristotle is lining him up for a key post if the election goes well?" Adonis asked her.

"That's the sixty-four-dollar question!"

Others in the newsroom disagreed. "No, it jolly well isn't!" Cicero said. "The big question is whether Caxton will quit as Editor if he gets such a post."

"If that happened, would Iago take over?" the youngest reporter asked.

"That's another leading question!" said Phaedra. "There are those who say he has had his eye on the job for a long time and, if given the chance, would stop at nothing to get it."

"I have heard another rumour that has been doing the rounds," said Adonis.

"Do you mean the one about Caxton having marital problems?" Phaedra asked.

"Why, what's he been up to?" an excited young reporter asked.

Phaedra gave him a conspiratorial look. "It's not what Caxton's been up to, it's his wife. I have heard it said that she has been playing away!"

"Who's been saying that?" Cicero asked irritably. He hated tittle-tattle at the best of times.

"It emanated from Iago, if I remember correctly."

Cicero bristled. "And do you really believe him?" he asked angrily. "I would trust Iago as far as I would a lump of rancid cheese!"

Adonis leaped to Phaedra's defence. "All right, let's calm down," he pleaded. "All Phaedra was saying was that it was a rumour. We have no way of knowing if it's true."

Cicero refused to be placated. "It could just as easily be a downright lie!"

"All right, all right!" Phaedra said with a pained expression. "Perhaps we should change the subject."

Adonis then said to Cicero: "Perhaps you could tell us what we are allowed to talk about!"

The only mouse in the room who failed to detect the tone of sarcasm was the youngest reporter, who suggested: "How about the elections?"

"Or, better still, there's that expedition," said Cicero. "How are they getting on? Where are they now? Why isn't the radio working when one of the explorers is a dab hand at fixing them? When, if ever, are we going to make contact again?"

Now it was Gertrude's turn to have her ire raised. "Aren't you all forgetting something?" she asked. "We've got one of our own out there on a dangerous mission, quite possibly putting his own life on the line. Doesn't anyone care about that?"

"I care," the youngest reporter said. "Marcus might not say much and doesn't mix much, but at least he's got the guts to go out and do it!"

"I care, too," said Cicero. "I care a great deal, in fact. And I'll tell you something else: there's a lot more to Marcus than most mice think."

"He was at the same school as us, if I remember correctly," Adonis said.

"Yes, he was, though I never knew him there, of course,

because of the age difference. I gather he didn't stay at the 'Cheese and Wheat' that long."

"He didn't," Adonis confirmed. "I didn't have any dealings with him myself, but I've heard that he didn't really fit in and was given a bit of a rough ride."

"I wonder what happened after he left the 'Cheese and Wheat'," Cicero mused.

"I can tell you that… or at least some of it," said Gertrude, who reminded everyone in the room that she was a Trojan and proud of it. "He had to leave that school after his father died and go back to Troy, which was his hometown, and go to another school that was far less posh."

"That must have been difficult for him," said Cicero.

The news desk secretary welcomed the opportunity to be the centre of attention. "That's an understatement!" she said. "He had two very difficult parents, who are now both dead. They were both extremely hard to please, especially his father, who berated him for not being as clever as he was. His mother, who committed suicide when he was very young, was plain loopy, by all accounts."

"How do you know all this?" Phaedra asked.

"We lived in the same street for a while. My parents knew his parents slightly, and I also heard various things about him from his schoolmates."

"Was he ostracised for being at a posh school in Phoenix?" Cicero asked.

"Yes, I gather he was. He had a pretty miserable time altogether."

"How did he get on with the females?" Phaedra asked.

Gertrude could not resist a smirk. "Now you're asking!" she exclaimed. "What I can tell you is that he used to be small, slight and not much to look at. But, on approaching adolescence, he shot up in height and filled out, too, and… er… became quite handsome."

The younger males in the room began to titter.

"Don't take any notice of them!" said Phaedra. "Do carry on!"

Gertrude grinned for a moment before offering a serious thought: "There's no doubt that he did attract some interest from the fairer sex. The trouble was that Marcus was so shy and gauche that he had no idea how to handle it."

"So, the females gave up?" Adonis suggested.

"Basically, yes. There were one or two who made their interest clear, and I believe he did have the odd date. But he was so inept socially, especially with the females, that nothing ever came of it."

"He never got married, did he?" Adonis observed.

"No, apparently not."

"I believe he went to a little-known university with no financial support and managed to get a First in English," Gertrude added. "After that, he landed a job on a small magazine."

"And then he got a job on a small newspaper, before getting a job here," said Phaedra, who was more than willing to fill the gaps.

"That's correct."

"So," said Phaedra, "that's the sad saga surrounding the life of Marcus, the timid explorer… who is perhaps not quite so timid as he makes out!"

"You've got quite a feature there for the paper!" Adonis remarked.

"Let's just hope he comes back and that you will then

write something that will do him justice," Cicero then said. "There's more to Marcus than you think. I'm sure of that."

Cicero's comments led to a moment of silence and reflection before an agitated Titus burst back into the newsroom. "We have lost all contact with the expedition," he announced. "All we can now do is wait and hope. Whatever happens next is in the lap of the gods."

CHAPTER 8

"*Wow!*"

Each member of the expedition party reacted in the same way on emerging from the hole and getting back into the open. Even Polo was stunned, not to mention dazzled, by what they saw. All four needed time to adjust to a degree of brightness they had never come across before. The need was amplified by the fact that they had just completed the most claustrophobic part of their journey.

They were at one end of a massive, flat area that was surrounded on all sides by towering mountains. It took them a while to realise this as, after every couple of minutes, sheets of light would appear and dazzle them. The sheets would sometimes split into segments, with multi-watt beams appearing to target specific areas. Sometimes, a beam would seem to be directed straight at the explorers, who were then obliged to cover their eyes and keep the light out the best they could.

Boxer was the first to speak: "Perhaps we should test the radio again?"

"Why not?!" Polo answered, with an air of indifference. He had been on many a trek before, some on his own, and had often not bothered with such an aid. The radio, this time, had been a late addition to Boxer's baggage after Titus, acting on instructions from Caxton, had expressly requested that it be taken.

Boxer fiddled with it fruitlessly before letting Rosencrantz have a go; if anyone could fix it, Rosencrantz could. However, this time he had to admit failure. "Dead as a door nail," he said. "It could simply be because we are so far away… or perhaps the unusual climate conditions have done it."

Polo shrugged his shoulders, prompting Boxer to ask him: "Shall I throw it away? You don't seem to care."

Polo was about to say, "Why not?!" again but changed his mind. "We'd better hang on to it, I suppose… as long as you don't mind carrying the damn thing!" Boxer, always willing to demonstrate his strength, assured Polo there was no problem.

Marcus, meanwhile, was preoccupied with the question of how to cope with the sheets and beams of light. "The sides of the mountains seem to be glistening," he said. "Glistening with gold!"

Polo nodded. "It's time for us to take a closer look… as long as we don't all go blind in the process!" he said. Every member of the expedition was squinting copiously.

Polo led the others down the gentle but slippery slope until the terrain became flat. The travellers were unable to identify what was underfoot, though they suspected they were walking on some kind of moss. The substance that covered the huge, flat area was much the same. The mountains to the left and right were more or less equidistant from where the quartet were walking, while whatever was directly ahead was much further away and barely visible. The sheets and beams of light were bearing down on them from all directions, apart from behind.

Polo suddenly remembered he had packed a couple of pairs of sunspecs-cum-goggles. "We can take turns at wearing these," he said. "They should help a bit, anyway." He put on a pair and handed the other to Rosencrantz. "OK, let's go!" he barked.

Polo started to lead the others along the vast plain, initially towards what looked like mountains that lay straight ahead but were many a mile away. The terrain was as flat as a pancake, but the going was slippery underfoot. Vegetation was non-existent, and the quartet remained unsure of what they were walking on. The ground was the colour of sand but not like sand in any other way. There was no wind, and the weather was neither hot nor cold. The area was massive. So, too, were the mountains that enclosed it on all sides and kept out any climactic elements that might prevail on the other sides of the mountains.

After half an hour of making no discernible progress, Polo called a halt and said: "We might do better going to one side."

"The light is blinding whichever way we go," Marcus commented.

"That's true," agreed Rosencrantz, "though I do believe we should turn either left or right… it doesn't seem to matter which."

"The mountains either side look exactly the same distance away as each other," said Boxer.

"They look the same as each other as well!" said Marcus.

After the shortest of pauses, Polo turned to the left and issued the order: "OK, let's go!"

Hours passed before the mountains to the left seemed to be any closer. Polo and Rosencrantz relinquished their eye coverings to give the other two some respite from the light.

None of the four really knew where they were going or what to expect, though the possibility of finding gold did much to sustain their resolve. That was, after all, one of the aims of the expedition, though by no means the only one. Polo had pointed out in the strongest possible terms that huge segments of the Isle of Andronicus remained undiscovered... and that was something he wanted to remedy. On top of that, he wanted to establish, once and for all, whether there had ever been some form of dominant civilisation before his own kind took over. That was a primary reason why he had wanted Marcus with him, as a substitute for Cicero who was not physically capable of coping with the rigours of the trip.

And there was yet another reason: to try to find out if there was, or ever had been, life outside Andronicus. Many a mouse scholar had expressed outrage at such a notion. There was only one world and mice reigned supreme, they had argued. Cicero, was known to be not so sure. Neither was Polo, a mouse with charisma coupled with a conviction that he had been born to seek out the truth in all things.

The small, stone bridge at the end of the tunnel had already provided a hint that the island might have, at some time, seen another civilisation.

On finally reaching the side of one of the mountains on the left, the quartet came upon another hint... an upwards path with steps. They did not see it immediately but, when they did, they could discern that a route had been carved out of a side of the mountain with the aid of tools of some sort.

A look of triumph spread across Polo's face. Although weary, wilting and, like the others, in need of a rest, he leaped into the air and proclaimed loudly: "Who said there was no point in going on this trip?!" The others cheered, and they all danced a little jig while looking upwards. Polo's exultation had put extra miles into the legs of all.

The quartet then sat down to eat and let the feeling of euphoria subside. "How are we for food?" Polo asked Rosencrantz, who had been given the task of keeping tabs on the substantial supply the four had set off with.

"We're all right for a while yet, though we will need to replenish our stocks at some point," the latter replied.

The upwards path seemed to go on forever. The steps were there to access the steeper parts. In many places, the path was extremely narrow and, with the light having an almost blinding effect at times, it was impossible to look either up or down. Polo – who was at the front and, at that point, wearing one of the two items of eyewear – told the others to take their time. The other three were more than willing to obey, though they all felt a sense of frustration as the mountainside continued to have a dark grey hue and showed no signs of going golden.

However, their patience was eventually rewarded. After ascending a long flight of steps that was virtually vertical, they reached a flat stretch that went to the right and for fifty yards skirted the mountainside and took the travellers to a mouse-sized hole. Just before the hole, the path was perilously narrow. Beams of light shone from it. Polo reiterated the need to take one's time in getting to it and squeezing through. For Boxer, this was no easy task. However, with a bit of pushing and pulling by the others, he managed it.

It was then a trip through a tunnel once more. Marcus was quick to quip about 'a feeling of déjà vu', though there were one or two subtle differences this time. The path, at this point, sloped steadily upwards and, every so often, there was a flight of steps to ascend. There was no need for torches, as the only visibility problems were caused by sudden flashes or beams of light. The third flight of steps, which was longer than the previous two, led to a sharp turning to the right, after which the walls dramatically changed colour. They ceased to be a dull dark grey and were instead a glistening gold.

The party came to an abrupt halt. The walls were lined with what looked like gold paint. The ceiling was gold, too. On closer inspection, however, it became apparent that nothing had been actually painted. The walls and ceiling were, in fact, partially covered by flecks and lumps of varying size, and the beams of light that shone from the sides and above and beyond had given the initial impression that fragments of gold had been melded together. Nearly all the pieces of gold, even the lumps, were tiny, and most of the pieces of any size were on or near the ceiling.

Boxer was the first to catch his breath. "Let me get at it!" he said, sounding more animated than anyone thought he could be. "I can soon find room for it." As Boxer eagerly opened the biggest rucksack and peered inside, Polo made a motion as if to say, 'hang on a minute!'.

Marcus then said: "Let's not rush anything. We should be taking a good look first. There's gold all over the place and we need to locate the best spot to get it from."

"Good thinking!" said Polo. "In any case, there is a limit to how much we can carry."

"I suppose we could always come back another time, now we know where it is," Rosencrantz suggested.

"I'll be up for that!" agreed Boxer, now seeing the sense of what the others said, though the idea of going through the rigours of the expedition all over again had never crossed his, or anyone else's, mind!

"Good!" said Polo. "And, yes, we can come back. In fact, we must. But let's not forget that we are not just here to find gold."

"But surely we can take some?!" a protesting Boxer said.

"Sure, we can," his leader confirmed. "But let's have a good recce first and concentrate on bringing back the best pieces we can."

The path continued to take the travellers towards the inside of the mountaintop. As it steepened, the concentration of gold deepened. The quartet eventually found a spot where there were lumps of gold the sizes of golf balls embedded in the ceiling and in one corner in particular. The spot was at the top of some steps, and everyone went to work.

One rodent had the task of placing the chisel near one of the lumps and holding it there, while another hit the chisel with a hammer. A third member held an open bag for the lump to fall into, while the fourth stood in a position where he could hopefully prevent anyone from falling. Everything was done at an awkward angle, and prising a lump away from where it was embedded took time and effort. The four took turns at all the tasks, until Polo eventually called halt with the words: "That's all, rodents! We've got fifteen beauties, and that should be enough for now."

The quartet wearily put down the hammer and chisel and packed away what they hoped would be new-found wealth.

"I wonder what gold is really worth... or whether it's worth anything," said Marcus.

"I don't know," Polo replied. "I don't think anyone knows, though Cicero and one or two others have this idea that it was once a highly valued commodity... and could be again."

Polo then asked Boxer if he had any problem with carrying the extra weight. "Don't worry about me – I'm fine!" was the reply. Boxer believed he had been brought into the world to lift and carry heavy weights. Polo suspected that he would have said he was fine even if he was on the verge of collapse. But he had to ask, anyway.

The expedition leader took a good look at all three of his companions and, with all his experience of travelling into the unknown and seeing how others could or could not cope with unfamiliar conditions, was satisfied that they had 'something left in the tank'. There was even a grin from Boxer.

"OK, it's onwards and upwards!" Polo declared. The path then steepened and narrowed, and the beams and flashes of light gradually disappeared, as did any trace of gold. Eventually, the path ended, and the four travellers were looking upwards at a gaping hole that was about ten feet above them. There were no steps to access the hole.

"I assume we have ropes," the resourceful Rosencrantz said. "Of course," replied Polo, who regarded such an item as a must for every journey, large or small. Without as much a word, Boxer assumed a squatting position to enable Polo to climb on to his shoulders. Rosencrantz passed the rope, which he had little trouble in finding, to Polo. The leader then tied one end to a nearby piece of rock.

CHAPTER 9

"Well, I'll be…" Polo was not easily surprised, but now he was almost at a loss for words.

"What's up?" Marcus asked from down below. "Are you all right?" At first, there was no answer.

"You have got us worried – what's the matter?" Rosencrantz called out.

"You'd better come up and see for yourselves," Polo said, after a pause.

The other three could not believe their eyes, either. For, standing in front of them was a shed-like structure that could not have been created by nature alone. A chill wind was blowing round it, and the travellers had to don extra clothing before thinking about inspecting it.

The structure was about twelve feet high, oblong in shape and clad in steel. A narrow, gravelled path ran along one side. It was considerably longer than initially expected, stretching a good hundred feet along what was clearly the top of a mountain. There were no windows. The quartet moved in single file along the path, taking care not to look down at the ravine that lay to the right. At the end, they could see the front of the structure, which had a large, padlocked front door. A hundred feet beyond the structure was an archway to another, smaller tunnel.

"So, perhaps we're about to see signs of life, after all," said Marcus, who, like the others, reflected on the fact that they had seen no such sign for days… not a mammal, not a bird, not a snake, not even an insect or a flower, and barely a blade of grass.

Then, just as Polo was about to give his customary, "On we go!" call, a sudden rustling sound, followed by a pattering of feet, could be heard. The sound of feet grew fainter until it could be heard no more. And there was no indication inside the small tunnel or on the path beyond of where it might have come from.

After about a hundred yards, the path dipped downwards for about a thousand feet towards another path that appeared to lead to another mountain. The descent turned out to be vertical in a couple of places, and Polo and his team were enthralled by the appearance of steps to make these parts easier to negotiate.

Even more enthralling was the appearance of a cave about halfway down. The cave mouth allowed access for one rodent at a time, but that was deceptive. The inside was massive, in terms of height, width and especially depth.

Polo switched on his most powerful torch and, almost immediately, gave a start. It was not so much the size that startled him as what was lying inside. To one side of the entrance, against a wall, was a large bag of grain. To the other were a table and six chairs, all folded and placed against another wall. In-between, a few feet away from the entrance, was a telescope mounted on a stool and appearing to be primed to observe anyone or anything for miles around. The inside of the cave, which was as spacious as the inside of a large house, appeared to be bare otherwise.

There were still more surprises in store. The light of the torch showed there were steps either side. The steps led to a series of wall-side paths, balconies and openings to places yet to be seen. Also unseen yet was the back of the cave, which, on inspection, looked as if it stretched endlessly into the mountain's bowels.

The travellers stood and stared at their surroundings before Polo echoed the thoughts of all by saying: "What an incredible place! There's so much to look at that it's difficult to know where to start." Rosencrantz suggested splitting into pairs, Polo agreed and Marcus, with tongue in cheek, offered to do the lower part because he was 'fed up to the teeth with going up and down steps!'. Polo turned to Marcus and said: "OK, I will go up with Rosencrantz and you can be with Boxer. Blow a whistle if you run into trouble, of course."

Marcus watched Polo and Rosencrantz scale the steps with the sort of agility he could only dream of possessing, before looking apprehensively towards where he and Boxer were to go. His companion waited impassively. The powerfully built hamster was happy in his role of baggage handler and follower.

The walk to the back of the cave took longer than expected, and it was several minutes before the walls began to close in and the ceiling became lower. Inevitably, perhaps, Marcus and Boxer arrived at the mouth of another tunnel. "It looks as if you made the wrong choice!" Boxer quipped, and Marcus could see the point. The tunnel was narrow and low, and there was going to be the need to stoop at times while going through it. Marcus winced a little, before saying: "It looks fine if you're four feet tall! Anyway, let's go!"

Meanwhile, more surprises awaited Polo and Rosencrantz. Once up one flight of steps, they could see that a passage ran along the length of each side wall and then ended. Three balconies protruded from each passage and looked down onto the cave floor. Most amazing of all, though, was the presence of a dozen doors each side that led to rooms which had clearly been carved out of stone. The rooms varied in size, and most were empty. However, a few of them contained small beds, tables, wardrobes and sinks. Two of the beds were unmade and looked as if they had just been slept in. At the far end of each passage was a bigger room containing a variety of items that included old furniture, a cooker that had seen better days and pieces of electrical equipment. All the rooms, empty or otherwise, had been kept clean and tidy.

The tunnel that Marcus and Boxer went through was mercifully short for a change, though Boxer in particular had to stoop nearly all the time. At the end was a wooden door with a handle. When Marcus turned the handle, the door would not move, and it quickly became apparent that it was bolted on the other side. Boxer gave the door a cramped shoulder charge but to no avail. The pair were about to give up when the sounds of sliding metal and pattering feet could be heard. Marcus turned the handle again and the door swung open gently.

The pair were greeted by the most incongruous sight imaginable. They stepped into what could best be described as a courtyard-cum-garden, though part of what they saw resembled a small field of thistles, nettles and assorted wild flowers, as well as grass. The whole area, which approached half an acre in size, was surrounded by high brick walls and shielded by a monolithic sheet of tarpaulin. The tarpaulin was held in place about twenty feet above the whole area by ropes affixed to a series of enormous trestles. Pebbled paths criss-crossed the area at various points and went round the entire perimeter as well. Some of the paths led to beds of flowers or other plants and also to a couple of fountains. In a far corner was a giant, flat structure that resembled a greenhouse.

Marcus and Boxer walked slowly round the perimeter, observing as they went that there were benches to sit on and a small, wooden table with four fold-up chairs leaning against it near one of the flower beds. They were eager to discover what lay inside the big, flat structure at the end, and even more keen to learn where the pattering of feet had come from. The flat structure, built almost entirely of glass, took up about fifty square feet. The glass, which sat on twelve inches of brick, was several inches thick and looked almost impossible to crack. "This must have taken some building!" Marcus whispered in something of an understatement. "Let's find out how we can get inside."

What happened next even startled the normally phlegmatic Boxer. For, just as the pair reached the next corner of the building, a throaty, high-pitched voice sang out: "Where are the other two?" A pattering of feet followed once more.

Marcus and Boxer spent the next few minutes looking in every direction but in vain. Marcus tried calling out: "Hello… we are friends. All we want to do is talk to you."

Boxer joined in with: "No one is going to hurt you."

Marcus then adopted a more pleading tone: "Please, show yourself. We have been travelling for days and days and not seen a soul. We just want to talk. Honestly!" Still no response.

After a pause, Marcus turned to Boxer and said: "I wonder where Polo and Rosencrantz have got to. Perhaps we should go back and look for them…"

Then, in almost the same instant, the pair miraculously appeared in the distance.

So, too, did a small shape… emerging from behind a garden gnome, of all things, before scuttling towards a wall, clambering up it and disappearing through an opening no one would have guessed existed. The four travellers gathered together as close to the hole as they could.

Polo called out and made another plea: "Please don't hide from us," he said. "All we want to do is talk to you as a friend." Eventually, a head, and then a pair of shoulders and the top half of a torso, appeared.

"Good grief!" Marcus murmured. "It's a rat!"

"My name is Odin," the rat said. "What do you want… er… I mean… what is it I can do for you?"

"I didn't know there were any of you left," Polo said.

"I suppose you wanted us all to be wiped out!" Odin retorted, with a first hint of aggression. "Sorry I have disappointed you!"

"We are not disappointed at all," Marcus said in a conciliatory tone. "Just surprised. Very surprised."

"We mean you no harm," Rosencrantz added.

Odin emerged fully from the hole he had been in, clambered down the wall and eyed the quartet nervously. "Don't come any closer!" he squeaked. The quartet could see he was barely four feet tall, dark brown in colour and had a slightly misshapen head. He was wearing blue dungarees and had a monocle protruding from a top pocket. "I first saw you coming several hours ago," he said. "You must have come a very, very long way."

Polo confirmed that they had, before adding: "I can't remember the last time we saw any signs of life."

"I hope you are not too disappointed that you have now seen a rat." Odin's quip seemed to have a touch of poignancy about it.

"Not at all," said Marcus. "Just surprised. I have seen pictures of rats before, but I must admit that I have never met one... until now." Polo then said he had encountered one or two on the outskirts of Phoenix but only while very young.

"So, you must have thought we had become extinct!"

"Maybe we did. But not now, that's for sure," Polo answered. "By the look of the set-up you have here, you must be part of a whole colony of rats?!"

Odin chuckled a little and then grew wistful. "That was the case once," he said. "The population was over a thousand at one time, though this was a long time before I was born. Most of my ancestors, and the ancestors of most of the rats who were born here, liked to live in towns. Life in towns was easy in those long-ago days... but then everything changed."

"What was it that changed?" Marcus asked.

"I am not sure I want to tell you," Odin replied. He began to look insecure and was poised to flee up the wall again.

Polo urged Odin not to worry. "Whatever happened in the past – and I have no idea what it was – you have nothing to worry about from us," he told him. "We are all delighted to see you, and we would like you to regard us as friends."

Odin was visibly relieved. "I would like that," he said. "I would like us to be friends. You can stay for a while as guests."

"That's tremendous! We would be delighted!" said Polo, who instinctively knew he was speaking for everyone. "Just one thing, though. We are running a bit low on provisions for our expedition, and we will have to find ways to stock up before long."

Odin managed a smile. "No problem," he said. "There's masses of stuff here. We have a surplus, in fact."

"Is some of it stored in the building we saw just before we entered the cave?" Marcus asked.

"Yes, quite a bit of it is in there, though there's more in there than just food."

"Like what?" asked a curious Polo.

"I will show you. I know you have seen quite a lot of this place already, but I can take you on a quick tour round all of it later on. I suggest a break and a bite to eat first, though."

"Sounds good to me!" said Boxer.

"I won't argue with that either!" Rosencrantz agreed. The other two smiled and nodded. Odin led the quartet to the tunnel they had all been through earlier and to the rooms that could be reached via the steps near the cave mouth. Four rooms with beds happened to be available for immediate occupation.

"Come back to where we first met in a couple of hours, and I will have a meal laid on for you," Odin instructed them all. "By the way… the place you are staying at is known as the Rats' Palace."

* * *

68

Marcus needed to be shaken by a shoulder after the two hours had passed. "Time for din-dins," a grinning Boxer told him, while standing over him.

"All right, give me a minute!" Marcus replied a little testily.

Marcus had not slept well. All the feelings of insecurity and self-doubt that had mounted up and loomed large for much of his life had swept over him as he lay on his bed. "What the heck are you doing in a place like this?" a voice in his head kept asking him. The voice had sounded like that of his father. Marcus had tried to come up with an answer, but he had stepped so far out of his comfort zone – intentionally, admittedly – that he could not find one. He had lain awake for an hour and a half, tossed and turned in the hope of finding a more comfortable position physically, and racked his brains in an attempt to make sense of it. In the end, exhaustion had made him lose consciousness.

He threw some clothes on and joined the others, who were waiting outside. "Come on, Sleepyhead!" Boxer said cheekily. "You're keeping us waiting, and I for one am ravenous!" Polo said he was more curious than hungry, and the four guests at the Rats' Palace all speculated on what lay in store for them as they made their way back to where they had first met Odin.

On emerging from the tunnel door, which had been left unlocked, they saw Odin standing beside a flower bed. Their host motioned them towards the big, glass building. As they approached, they saw a large, mahogany table with five matching chairs just outside the building. Mats, plates, glasses and neatly folded serviettes had been strategically placed on the table, too. "Come and sit down," Odin said to them.

As they did, two more rats appeared and stood with a subservient air nearby. One was old and the other young, and they were both wearing aprons. Neither of them was more than three feet tall. "Let me introduce you to Portia and Petal," said Odin. "They will be dining separately later and, for now, will be tending to our needs."

The older one, who turned out to be Portia, opened a wine bottle and poured a few drops into a glass for Odin to test and approve before filling up all five glasses to the top. Petal disappeared into the big building and, almost immediately, reappeared with a trolley laden with delicacies that included high-quality grain and some cheese. "We used to keep goats," Odin explained. "We will have plenty of cheese in stock, but these days, we tend to save it for special occasions... such as this."

"The cheese is really good," Marcus said later. "So are the grains, for that matter... and the wine is excellent. Presumably, you grow the grapes?" Odin confirmed this with a nod and then waved towards the big, glass building.

"What about your two helpers?" Marcus asked a few moments later. He instinctively knew that a little caution was called for now. "I had been under the impression earlier that you were living here on your own. Is there anyone else here, apart from you three?"

"No, it's just the three of us," Odin replied, looking distinctly uncomfortable. "The others died off."

"The Rats' Palace must have quite a history behind it," Marcus suggested. "How long has it been in existence? You said earlier that there used to be thousands of you. Why is that not so now?"

Odin looked decidedly unhappy. "All I can tell you is that

it was many generations ago. Rats were no longer welcome in the towns, or anywhere near them, and eventually they were all driven out."

"Why were rats suddenly unwelcome?" Marcus asked with uncustomary boldness. He knew he was pushing his luck.

"I have nothing else to tell you," replied Odin, who was now visibly angry. "Let's leave it!"

"We're sorry. We have no wish to offend you," said Polo, who found himself wearing the unfamiliar mantle of diplomat. "Marcus happens to be a journalist and, well, you must know what a nosy lot they are!"

Odin appeared far from convinced, though his expression did soften a little. He asked his guests if they would like to see the inside of the big, glass building.

CHAPTER 10

"Still no word from Marcus, I suppose?" Caxton asked Cicero, the mouse who seemed to know him the best.

"I'm afraid not," the veteran Feature Writer answered. Cicero sensed that his Editor would welcome answers on a number of issues, not the least concerning his own private life.

Caxton cursed, before asking anyone within hearing distance, but no one in particular, if they knew where Phaedra was.

"She's out on a job," Gertrude called out from the news desk. Titus assured him she would not be long.

Caxton then asked Titus about his plans for covering the elections. "I've got interviews arranged with the candidates regarding what they stand for and what they intend to achieve," the latter said. "Phaedra is chatting to some of the behind-the-scenes workers, and I plan to write a prediction piece myself."

"Fine!" said Caxton. "At least, it's fine as far as the elections go. Our problem is that we have nothing new on the expedition. I was hoping we would have heard something by now and had one or two reports in the bag. That would have given the *Standard* a bit more variety. As you know, I like to see lots of variety in the paper, especially when it's stuff about *rodents!*"

"I'm afraid we're stuck there," said Titus. "And at the rate things are going, or perhaps I should say not going, Marcus won't be back before the start of the Cold Season."

"You've got a point," Caxton said. "He'll be battling with the elements while the rest of us are underground."

"Perhaps we should have a 'stopgap' piece of some sort lined up, just in case."

Caxton nodded. "Yes, I think we should do that. Get Phaedra to report to me as soon as she gets back."

All eyes were on Caxton as he left the newsroom. As soon as he had gone, and thought to be well out of earshot, one of the reporters observed that there was 'a mouse with much on his mind'.

"He doesn't seem to be quite his usual self," another agreed. "He's lost a bit of his bounce, somehow."

"I wouldn't want to complain about that!" the first one said. "Perhaps his wife should play away more often!"

"Come off it!" said Gertrude. "We don't even know if it's true."

"Who started the rumour, anyway?" the first reporter asked.

"I believe it was Iago," said Cicero, sounding a little irritated. "The question, surely, is whether you can trust anything Iago says."

"Point taken!"

Titus was irritated, too. "You need to keep your voices down," he warned. "Sound carries further than you think, and you never know who might be listening just outside."

At that very moment, Phaedra flounced in. "Hello!" she said, with a conspiratorial air. "Have I been missing something? Has a new juicy scandal come to light?"

Titus cut the conversation short. "His Nibs wants words with you, pronto!" he told Phaedra.

"Perhaps he needs comforting!" she quipped. Titus responded with an exasperated wave towards Caxton's office door.

After knocking on the door and obeying a curt call to enter, Phaedra was told to sit, and the Editor got straight to the point. "Have you got any ideas for an extra feature – a stopgap feature – in case we get nothing from Marcus?"

"No, not apart from what I'm doing already," a slightly nonplussed Phaedra replied. She noticed that the worry lines on Caxton's face had become more pronounced.

"There must be something!" Caxton exclaimed desperately. "It doesn't matter if it's light-hearted or trivial. We need something to get the balance of the paper right."

Phaedra paused for a moment, during which she recalled a recent discussion among colleagues on the subjects of snobbery and class distinction. "How about a piece on what social class we all belong to?" she suggested.

"Does anyone care these days?"

"Well, I don't, and there are probably only a few who do, but I could, I suppose, give the whole social standing thing a bit of a send-up."

"All right," said Caxton, rubbing his chin. "Do it tongue in cheek and give the readers something to laugh about. That's it… we can show everyone that the rodents of Phoenix, and the *Standard* in particular, can laugh with the best of them!"

* * *

Phaedra found the task of being amusing on this occasion something of a drudge. She regretted having made the suggestion as soon as she was back in her office. What was there to say? Who would be interested? She felt she had made a misjudgement and that, incredible as it may seem, her Editor had as well. *That's not like him at all*, she thought. Caxton had been criticised many a time for seeming to like to hive off work to others and leave them to sort out the details. His loudness and bluster did not always go down well, either. But when it came to deciding what was best for the *Standard*, he had never put a foot wrong... until now. Had problems with his private life, assuming they existed, impaired his judgement?

In the meantime, Phaedra needed to stay in Caxton's good books. She had managed to oust Cicero, who had clashed with Caxton once too often from his position as Features Editor. But she could not afford to make a hash of her latest task, let alone refuse to do it, as there was always the possibility of it being assigned to the more experienced Cicero instead. If that happened, her entire standing at the *Standard* could be in jeopardy. So, she began to focus on the facts she was aware of.

There were different breeds of mice living on the Isle of Andronicus, including the House Mouse, Field Mouse, Harvest Mouse and Yellow-Necked Mouse. More than ninety per cent of those who were not a mixture belonged, in almost exactly equal numbers, to either of the first two categories, while just under nine per cent were Harvest Mice. They all enjoyed much the same social standing, though, in some quarters, Yellow-Necked Mice were considered inferior because they were unusual. Much the same could be said about mixed-breed mice, though precious few cared.

There was said to be intense dislike between the inhabitants of Phoenix and Troy, and perhaps those from other locations, but this had been written about many times already. Different breeds of mice differed in colour, but so what? The same could be said of the fact that different mouse types tended to like different food.

Lower down the social scale, of course, were gerbils, hamsters and shrews... in that order. As rodents, they were at least able to walk on their hind legs, and they were certainly superior to other types of mammal. Segregation between rodents had been consigned to the past, and they were now all allowed to use the same facilities, such as pubs, cafes and public conveniences. In practice, though, the doors to the best schools and jobs were closed to them. A couple of gerbils had admittedly gained places in the Mouse Police a year ago, and this was a big story at the time. Hamsters were valued for their ability to carry out menial tasks and often for their strength. Shrews, on the other foot, were regarded as bad-tempered and unreliable, and they were a dying – if not dead – breed, anyway.

Phaedra then reflected on what she had read about rats and voles. She knew little about the latter, except that they had rarely lived in urban areas.

Rats, on the other foot, were predominantly town dwellers in the days of yore. Why they had ever been attracted to towns was unclear. All Phaedra knew was that something happened to make their numbers dwindle and that the rats remaining in towns had been driven out of them and, on the face of it, to extinction.

There had been the belief that rats had not died out completely and, because that particular subject had not been covered for a while, Phaedra considered writing a piece on 'Are There Still Rats About?'. The problem with that, however, was that she would almost certainly have to consult Cicero, an accomplished rodent historian with a strong interest in the subject himself.

In the end, she managed to cobble together some words on 'Rodent Supremacy', which included profiles of the island's most charismatic inhabitants as examples of mousehood at its best. Special mentions were made of Polo, Da Vinci and, inevitably, Caxton.

CHAPTER 11

"Something tells me you're going to be moving on soon," Odin said to Polo. Almost everything Odin said was now addressed to the same rodent. He did not trust Marcus and liked him even less when he realised he was writing something in a notebook at every opportunity. Rosencrantz and Boxer, already aware of their stations in life, stayed in the background and kept a low profile.

"There are still things we are keen to discover," Polo said.

Odin was leading his guests round the big, glass building, which contained an array of flowers and ornamental shrubs, as well as cereal plants and fruit-bearing bushes. "As you can see, we are totally self-sufficient," he said. "We do, in fact, have something of a glut of most things at present, and you are welcome to relieve us of some of our produce and take it on your travels." Polo thanked Odin profusely.

"You will have noticed that the temperature is slightly higher here than in the rest of the Rats' Palace... yes? We can turn the heat up and down when we want to, though we rarely do."

Odin then paused before saying, with some pride: "What you might *not* have noticed is that the temperature in the rest of the Palace is constant… though we can regulate that as well, if we want to."

"What happens with the temperature, and the climate generally, outside?" Polo asked.

"It depends where you are. If you are on the top of a mountain, it can be pretty cold. Stormy, too. Lower down, it's much milder."

Polo made reference to the four seasons, with distinct climactic differences, that he was accustomed to.

"I have heard about that, though I can't remember where from," Odin said. "The weather round here does not change that much. I must admit, though, that I rarely travel any distance these days. So, I don't really know what it's like on other parts of the island."

Marcus was about to ask whether rats travelled further afield in the past but decided it was best for him to keep his counsel just now.

Polo told Odin how impressed he was with the big, glass building and, indeed, with the Rats' Palace as a whole. "It must have taken a heck of a lot of work. How much of a paw did you have in its creation?"

"Just a little," Odin replied. "Much of it was here before I was born, though I have been involved with the upkeep of just about everything here all my life."

"The upkeep must be a job and a half itself."

"I did lay some of the paths you have been walking on, come to think of it. I also helped build the steps to the bedrooms and storage areas near the cave entrance."

"Those rooms must have come in handy."

"Yes, they have, though not so much recently. I hope everyone found the rooms they slept in comfortable." Odin then suggested that now was a good time to take his guests on the tour he had promised. The quartet acquiesced readily.

As it turned out, they had seen most of what they were shown already. However, there was a surprise or two. The first was the presence of a few holes in the sides of the tunnel that took them back to the cave entrance. Each hole had a door to it and enough room inside for an adult rat to enter and sit. The doors were the same colour as the walls and were only visible to those aware of their existence and actively looking for them. "Good for hiding in," Odin said. Similar 'hidey-holes' could be found in various parts of the cave area, including in some of the bedrooms.

"Does the telescope near the cave mouth get used much?" asked Marcus, who had decided to break his silence and satisfy his curiosity.

Odin stared upwards at the face of the mouse he did not trust and said coldly: "Yes, we do use it. Even now. We know when someone is coming a lot sooner than you might think."

Odin gave the quartet time to admire the rugged scenery that could be viewed from the cave mouth, before drawing attention to a variety of ladders kept in a storage cupboard. "These can be used for all sorts of purposes, ranging from getting to places that need cleaning, to helping us to get out in a hurry," he said.

"Why would you need to?" Rosencrantz asked.

Odin ignored the question and instead pointed upwards. "We even have holes in the ceiling where it is possible to hide or, if necessary, make an escape. The escape route to the top is not ideal, but it's a case of needs must."

"So, I take it that won't be the way we're going to leave?!" said Polo.

"Oh, no, I have something far better in store for you. Anyway, let's not be too hasty. I am hoping you will enjoy our hospitality for at least another day or two. I hope you have all found your sleeping quarters satisfactory."

"They're fine," his four guests said in unison.

At this point, Marcus could not resist asking another question: "Where do you live and sleep yourself? And what about Portia and Petal?"

"Why do you ask?" Odin responded with a stony look.

"I'm sorry," said Marcus, who realised he had been treading on eggshells. "As Polo said, I am just a nasty journalist who's having the experience of a lifetime and wants to learn from it."

"And write about it!"

"Yes, and write about it! My readers will be most interested to learn about our expedition and what we have discovered. Is that really so bad?"

"Will what you write be anti-rat?"

Marcus was genuinely gobsmacked for a moment. "Absolutely not!" he eventually said in a tone that was not lost on anyone. "I have never written anything that would harm any kind of rodent, and I am not going to start now."

"We want to be your friends," Boxer added.

Boxer's assertion in particular seemed to strike a chord with Odin, whose attitude softened markedly. The edgy air disappeared and, at last, Odin looked relaxed and at ease. "All right, I will tell Portia and Petal that they have no reason to fear you," he said quietly. "I will also show you where the three of us live, and I am sure the other two will be glad to talk to you once I have had a word with them."

"That would be wonderful, as long as you have no objection," said Polo. "Are you sure you are happy with that? We don't want to put anyone in a difficult position." Odin assured him that everything was fine, and the others murmured their thanks.

"Before we do that, there's something else I would like to show you," Odin then said.

Without waiting for an answer, he led his guests to a large cupboard close to the corridor entrance, opened the door to it and removed its contents. At the back of the cupboard was another, smaller door which Odin opened and went through. He motioned the others to follow. Once they were all through, the quartet were able to stand upright. Odin switched on a torch, which illuminated a passage that sloped upwards.

"This will be your way out of here," he said. "The path ahead of you will take you to the mountaintop and towards the northern part of the island, which you have yet to see. The journey is likely to be hazardous, and I will not blame you if you decide to forget it and go back the way you came instead."

"There's no going back now," Polo said. "That is not an option." Odin nodded as if to acknowledge that there was no point in trying to persuade his guests that it was. "We would like to take you up on your offer to show us where you live and for us to talk to Portia and Petal, though," Polo added.

Odin smiled. "No problem! And stick around for as long as you like!"

Odin then suggested that his guests go to their rooms for a while and join the three rats for a meal later. "I think the other two will be joining us at the table this time," he said.

* * *

The two females were surprisingly animated when the six rodents all got together at last. A table had been laid for six, and a meal consisting of cheese, oats and assorted berries was enjoyed. And the atmosphere was relaxed. Petal, who was in her early adolescence, giggled almost endlessly. Portia, who was the oldest of the diners by far, regaled the guests with amusing anecdotes. All traces of shyness had disappeared. The only hints of seriousness while all were eating arose when Petal tried to make light of the difficulty she faced in finding a male suitor and Portia alluded to the days when the Rats' Palace was populous.

"I believe you would like to see where we all live," Portia said once the meal was over and the table had been cleared. Marcus observed how small and frail-looking the two females were, even compared with Odin, and made a mental note of that.

"Perhaps you would like to lead the way," Odin said to Portia.

The latter caressed an area of wall close to the big, glass building and a door slid open to reveal an area of space beyond it. "You would never have known it was there, would you?" she said with a triumphant smile, before walking through. Once all six rodents were inside, Portia pressed a button near the opening, and the door slid shut. A click of a nearby switch then turned on a light, which revealed a long, steep staircase. "Follow me," said Portia. Unfortunately, getting to the top was a struggle for her, and the others wondered how much longer she would be able to tackle the stairs.

At the top was a landing with three bedrooms, a small kitchen and a bathroom. The rooms were all in an area which had been cut out of the mountain at some point. As Portia fought to get her breath back, Odin apologised to her for not leading the guests upstairs himself. He then said: "As you can see, the bedrooms are similar to the ones you have been sleeping in. More importantly, it's impossible to find us here."

"Smashing, isn't it?!" exclaimed an exuberant Petal.

"Most impressive!" Polo agreed. "I haven't ever seen anything quite like this before." Polo turned to Marcus, who was wearing one of his quizzical looks, and asked him what he thought.

"It's quite incredible," Marcus added. "If you need somewhere to hide, you couldn't do better."

"Something tells me you want to know why anyone should want to hide," Odin said to Marcus with a knowing look. "Perhaps Portia is the one best qualified to enlighten you on this."

Portia, who had just about regained her breath, said: "I will tell you what I can."

Marcus asked a little nervously if it was all right for him to take notes, and Odin told him to go ahead.

"We have a lot of enemies," Portia said. "At least, we used to and probably still do."

"Like who?" Boxer asked incredulously.

"You may not know this, but a lot of rats used to live in towns," Portia continued. "You might wonder why they don't anymore. Well, the reason is simple: they were driven out and killed in huge numbers... by... *mice*! You might understand now why we were so reluctant to talk about this until we got to know you a bit."

"So, that is why rats retreated to the countryside?!" Marcus interjected.

"Yes, that's right, but that was not the end of the story. The mice continued to hunt the rats down, and they tried to wipe them out completely. They might well have succeeded had it not been for the fact that some of the rats retreated to the mountains and eventually found this place. As you are well aware, the Rats' Palace is pretty remote, and the chasing mice simply assumed that their victims had disappeared without trace."

"So, the rats formed a colony here?"

"Yes, they did, and for a time, things went fine. The rat population grew and flourished. Then, two really bad things happened. Firstly, the rats had to defend their territory against an army of shrews, and secondly, not long afterwards, there was a flu epidemic.

"During the first crisis, the shrews were all killed, as far as I know, and a lot of rats lost their lives as well. The flu epidemic caused even more deaths. I was very young, younger than Petal is now, when that happened, and I saw all my relatives succumb. When it was all over, there were just a dozen of us left. I am the only one remaining out of that dozen, and as you can see, there are now just the three of us."

Marcus considered asking how the decimated rat population fared after the epidemic but was stopped by a stern look from Odin and a loss of composure by Portia. The latter suddenly burst into tears, dashed into a bedroom, locked the door and could be heard sobbing uncontrollably.

CHAPTER 12

A fond farewell was accorded to the guests as Odin opened the door of the cupboard near the corridor that was to lead them to the next stage of their expedition. Petal blew kisses to all of them and called out, "Come again soon!" as they moved towards the upward passage.

The quartet had enjoyed four days of hospitality at the Rats' Palace and were, in many ways, reluctant to leave. They had been wined, dined and treated like VIMs. Petal had bombarded them with questions about where they were going, where they had been and, above all, what life was like for them back home. She even asked if she could join the expedition and whether she could see the guests again in Phoenix or elsewhere. Odin had smiled knowingly and, at times, shaken his head. Portia had remained invisible for most of the time and had only reappeared briefly to wish the travellers well on their journey.

Polo and the others voiced appreciation for the way they had been treated and expressed special gratitude for the food, clothing, and other bits and pieces such as extra torches and batteries they had been given to take with them.

Odin made particular reference to the woolly hats and insulated underwear he had handed over. "Where you are going is going to be colder, with the conditions more hostile than anywhere you have been before," Odin said. "I have travelled a short way in that direction but was forced back by a blizzard. It would not surprise me if you ended up the same way."

Odin's words echoed in the quartet's ears as they began their ascent. They had become pretty adept at negotiating narrow passages by now, but this latest one turned out to be the most challenging yet. It was dark, dank, sometimes slippery underfoot, extremely cold and, at times, almost vertical. After travelling just a few feet, the darkness became almost total. Four powerful torches, donated by Odin, were fished out and handed to Rosencrantz. The resourceful gerbil found a way of fixing them onto the fronts of four items of head gear so that the beams of light from them could shine to the front and enable the travellers to make effective use of crampons when they were needed.

The journey through the passage took literally hours and seemed even longer! Polo took the lead, followed by Rosencrantz and the less agile Marcus and Boxer. Marcus slipped backwards several times, and Boxer needed all his strength to help him regain his footing and push him forwards. Boxer had trouble himself when the passage narrowed a couple of times, and he had to battle to squeeze through. Polo, meanwhile, had to contend with pieces of loose earth and shale ahead of him that fell in his face without warning… and was sometimes deflected on to Rosencrantz below.

Just as the quartet were beginning to believe that their ordeal was going to last forever, and were even thinking about Odin's plea for them to abandon their journey, Polo espied a chink of light ahead and then a tiny hole. The hole took twenty minutes to reach and turned out to be far too small to pass through. "This might be all right for Odin, but none of us will ever get through that," said Polo. "Who's got a hammer and chisel?!" Boxer fished out one of each and passed them up. Polo warned the others to mind their heads before going to work on widening the opening.

The roar of the wind intensified, and the sky blackened as Polo worked. A single sheet of lightning was blinding for a moment, but then it provided Polo with a picture of what lay ahead and an idea of where the quartet were. They were at the top of a mountain they had been climbing through and within sight of the peaks of several others. Directly ahead was a narrow ridge that led to a hole in a slightly higher peak. There appeared to be a sheer drop on either side of the ridge, though Polo was not entirely sure at this stage. The lightning was gone within seconds and the sky darkened to such an extent that Polo could barely see three feet of ridge. "We are going to have to wait here for a while," he told the others.

The quartet had no option but to remain in their positions, which were far from comfortable, and wait in the hope that conditions would improve. A massive thunderclap followed the lightning. The whole of the mountain they were inside shuddered and, for a moment, gave the impression that it was about to topple. Then, remarkably, silence reigned, the darkness ended and the sky lost its anger.

Not surprisingly, Polo waited for a while to see what else the forces of nature might bring. "Is everyone all right down there?" he asked the others.

"As well as can be expected!" Marcus answered ruefully. "It's not exactly luxurious down here, though, and I for one won't be sorry to be moving on."

Polo looked at the ridge again. "It shouldn't be long now... and I hope you won't be eating your words!" he said.

Polo waited until he was reasonably sure that another storm or some other climactic surprise was not imminent before deciding it was as safe as it ever would be to proceed. He told Boxer and Marcus to be linked together by a rope. He could now see that the ridge was the length of about ten average houses and that, because it was too narrow to walk along, it would have to be straddled.

Although still remarkably agile, Polo was conscious of the fact that he was not young any more and he did not relish the next task. He had to set an example, though, and with trepidation, he mounted the ridge in much the same way as he would mount a bicycle. With a leg dangling either side, he slowly propelled himself forwards. Rosencrantz followed, once Polo was halfway across. He was almost as agile as his leader, and there was little that held fear for him. So, slowly but surely, he, too, completed a task that many a rodent would not even contemplate.

The other two were less agile, but Boxer was totally fearless, and Polo was reasonably confident that he could get across in his own time and help Marcus in the process. His insistence on having Boxer and Marcus roped together was more than justified. Progress for the pair was painstaking, and there were several occasions when Marcus came close to falling down one side. Towards the end of the journey across, he did just that and Boxer used the rope and his strength to haul him to safety. The time they took to traverse the ridge was inevitably far longer than it was for Polo and Rosencrantz.

There were sighs of relief all round when the ordeal was finally over. Marcus was in a state of collapse, and Polo ruled that another rest was called for. The rest turned out to be a long one, and the *Standard* journalist could not conceal his embarrassment. "I am really sorry to have held you all up," he said shamefacedly. Rosencrantz assured him he had nothing to worry about.

"What you did took guts," Boxer added.

Polo nodded and, hard-boiled though he could be, told Marcus: "You've got guts aplenty!"

Before moving on, the four travellers refreshed themselves by eating some of the berries that Portia and Petal had picked and packed for them. They were sitting in a small, elongated cave-cum-tunnel with an opening at the far end. The opening led to a narrow path that sloped slightly downwards to another opening. There was a steep drop on either side of the path, but this time it was possible to walk along it in single file. The opening provided access to another cave and another path. The path sloped slightly upwards this time and, again, led to a cave.

Further paths and caves were encountered that day, and the next, as the expedition progressed. Some of the paths sloped upwards, some down, but they were all of similar length and they all overlooked rocky crevices. The caves were of similar size and shape and proved to be adequate places for sleeping. Winds came and went but were less savage than those that greeted the quartet when they emerged from the mountaintop hole. Rain clouds opened a couple of times and gave the travellers a soaking, though they all agreed that, if anything, conditions were becoming more manageable.

From then on, the weather gradually got warmer. The sky lost its greyness and turned blue. Fluffy white clouds adorned it, but these gradually became fewer and, little by little, were replaced by increasing numbers of red flecks. This scenario prevailed for the best part of a week, before a dramatic change took place.

It happened after a customary 'cave break'. The latest cave was longer than the others encountered since leaving the Rats' Palace and, unlike the others, was L-shaped, with an exit lying sharply to the right. The path to the exit sloped upwards. The quartet noticed that the temperature, which had been rising gradually for several days, was now going up sharply. Once outside, they could see why.

On the horizon was a volcano throwing red embers into the sky. The sky immediately above it was red. Elsewhere, it was dominated by red flecks. Between the cave and the volcano was a grassy plain, bounded to the left and right by green hills. The grass near the cave was luxuriant. Away from the cave, it was brown, black or non-existent depending on its proximity to the embers.

"Volcanoes can hold secrets," said Polo. "Let's see how close we can get." Before anyone could ask what he meant, or what those secrets could be, the quartet were on the move.

Perhaps he's just looking for a reason to carry on, Marcus thought. *The only reason I can think of is that the only alternative is to go back.*

As they drew closer to the volcano, the air turned acrid, eyes began to smart and lungs to heave. The hills to the side were darkening almost as quickly as the grass the quartet were walking on.

Rosencrantz espied a gap in the hills to the right and,

as soon as the gap was drawn to his attention, Polo turned towards it and the others unquestioningly followed. The change of direction could hardly be more disagreeable than where they were going before.

The gap revealed an upwards path that led to two tunnels. The one to the left went sharply towards, or perhaps slightly to the left of, the volcano. The other, angled at about forty-five degrees to the right, went away from it. "Let's go left," said Polo. "If the going gets too hot, we can always go back to the other path."

Torches were needed and, although the path was reasonably smooth, progress was slow. The air was thin and breathing laboured, though no more so than when the gap in the hill was first seen. "My guess is that we're skirting the side of the volcano," said Rosencrantz. "I won't be sorry to see the other side!" said Marcus.

Marcus, who was at the back, then almost lost his footing as he failed to spot a loose stone and dropped his torch. On stooping to pick the torch up, he saw something the others had missed and gave a start. "Are you all right?" Polo called back. Marcus said he was fine but asked the others to stop for a minute.

Marcus shone his torch on to a section of wall to the right, close to where he had tripped. The beam of light from the torch revealed a small handle at just above knee height. He pulled the handle with all his might until a door slid open to expose a gap just big enough for a mouse to get through.

Inside was a well-like hole that was about twenty feet deep. A series of rungs led to the bottom. Marcus shone the torch onto an earthen floor and could not conceal his excitement when he saw what appeared to be a massive, leather-bound book and two long, rolled-up scrolls of paper. "I've got to go down," he said. "Someone hold my torch, please."

Polo would have normally insisted on going down first himself. But he was so taken aback by the sudden audacity of the least experienced, supposedly most timid, member of the group that he simply urged caution. "Take your time," he said. "Make sure the rungs are secure."

The reinforced leather-bound book took up almost half of the space at the bottom and was too heavy for Marcus to lift. He was hard put to move the front cover, in fact, and when he did, he saw that most of the pages were blank. Other pages featured what appeared to be maps and drawings, as well as words that had faded so badly that they were indecipherable. The scrolls, which the years seemed to have treated more kindly, kept springing back into their rolled-up position when Marcus tried to make them flat and read what had been written on them. "Can someone join me with a camera and some light?" he eventually pleaded.

Polo quickly joined him and, working together, the pair were able to open the scrolls and take a proper look. Unfortunately, the words turned out to be gobbledegook and the illustrations, if that is what they were, were so faint that they looked like nothing more than shadowy blobs. "We are going to have to run these past someone like Cicero to try to get them deciphered," said Marcus.

The pair then examined the book, which, when open, left them little room to stand. The pages had faded badly, though they featured the same sort of gobbledegook that was on the scrolls. There were also ancient maps, which had become disjointed. And barely visible to the naked eye were a couple of drawings of strange creatures that stood on hind legs but bore no resemblance to rodents.

"This is quite a discovery," said Polo. "It might even be a major part of why we are here." He patted Marcus gently on the back and added with a wink: "Now you know why I chose you for this trip!"

Polo photographed some of the pages in the book and picked up the scrolls, which he carried to the hole where the others were waiting. An elated Marcus closed the book, which was clearly too heavy and bulky to take where they were going. He lifted up the fortified front cover and let it drop down to where it was before. The impact led to a cloud of dust appearing in an angry haze. The dust flew into Marcus's eyes, nose, ears, mouth and throat, causing him to cough, sneeze, wheeze and scream before losing consciousness.

CHAPTER 13

Everything was urgent when the Temperate Season was about to end. There were two weeks left, perhaps three, and almost all the rodents of Phoenix, Troy, Carthage and other settlements within reach of these towns knew that now was the time to get ready to go below ground. They knew there would be a stern warning before the arrival of the Cold Season. It would come in the form of an icy blast and an early morning redness in the sky. The icy blast would last for anything between an hour and a day, and it would leave those who felt it in no doubt that the temperature was about to plummet.

Municipal workers went into overdrive to ensure that anything not wanted underground would be cleared away and, at the same time, stow away or otherwise protect objects above ground when necessary. Making sure that underground transport would continue to run efficiently was another crucial task, as was the checking of utilities such as water, drainage and electricity.

Most of the Andronicus Cold Season homes were below ground, though some of the wealthier mice had second or third properties that were on stilts. These needed to be kept secure and storm-proof. However, some of the rural dwellers, and a handful of urban eccentrics, preferred to live above ground, and for them, battening down the hatches became imperative.

For politicians and newspaper reporters, the sense of urgency became magnified. Canvassing ahead of the elections that were due to take place on the known parts of the island had added to the feverishness of the atmosphere. On top of this, reporters were busy with interviews, predictions and coverage generally. The elections on the island took place every four years and this year, they were expected to be more closely contested than ever.

The two main political factions were the Status Quo Party and the Right the Wrongs Initiative, otherwise known as RTWI or The Rebels. Other groups, such as Gerbils' Rights and Keep the Island Green would field candidates in some constituencies. Ten of these were in Phoenix, seven in Troy, four in Carthage and the other four in far-flung locations. The fact that Phoenix had more constituencies than anywhere else was a constant source of anger for many Trojans.

Each constituency would be represented by three councillors, with each council candidate appointed by members of the political group concerned. A group leader, however, would be decided upon following votes by fellow councillors. The councillors were part of the Andronicus Parliament, with the leader of the group winning the election becoming Prime Minister. As island leader, the PM had the power to appoint other councillors to various executive posts, such as Minister of Wealth, Head of the Crime Bureau and Chief Weather Watcher.

Representatives of each political group had been campaigning feverishly for support, with radio broadcasts, driving around with loud hailers, canvassing and delivering leaflets.

The Status Quo Party was expected to win yet again, though, on this occasion, only just and not without a fight. There was still the odd die-hard in the party who believed in divine rights for upper-class male mice, but they were a rarity now and members had had to adjust their stance considerably over the years. There had even been talk of changing the party's name.

The Rebels, who had managed to secure votes for female mice in an earlier campaign, were now pressing for better housing for the lower classes, equal educational opportunities and more rights for inferior rodents. With support from Gerbils' Rights, they had recently managed to get Parliament to enfranchise nominated gerbils who had excelled in sport, scholastic endeavour or outstanding service to the community. Among those to have benefitted was Rosencrantz, whose name had been put forward by the influential Polo. Extending such a concession to hamsters was now under review, with the case of Boxer, a renowned athlete as well as an intrepid explorer, being cited as a deserving example.

The polling booths had just opened, and with voting compulsory, the queues were mounting. Lifts by buggy to the booths were being offered to the infirm and others who might find it difficult to get to them, and it was not unusual for a voter living 'out in the sticks' to receive simultaneous offers from rival factions. Voting was allowed to continue until well after nightfall, after which the counting would start.

Activity among members of the media was almost as frenzied as it was among politicians and their supporters. At the *Phoenix Standard*, Titus was as stressed as ever. Once again, he was in charge of the newspaper's 'Election Special'. He knew that any kind of glitch would be deemed from above as his fault.

Caxton, who had decided to stand as an Independent in the elections and was relying on his charisma to secure a seat, was rarely around. His wrath, when incurred, could be colourful, though contact with the Editor this time round was likely to be minimal. This meant having to report to Iago, a mouse who rarely raised his voice but exuded menace, nonetheless.

Iago was tall, lean and something of a social outsider. He did not come from a wealthy or well-bred family and had lived most of his life in a down-at-heel and peripheral Phoenix neighbourhood. He had risen to his position of Deputy Editor by dint of hard work, a fine academic record and a punctilious approach to everything he did. He did not suffer fools at all and at the *Standard* was known as a mouse not to be crossed.

Iago's relationship with Caxton was purely professional as the newspaper's two top editorial executives had little in common. The Editor respected his deputy's dedication and his ability to dot i's and cross t's but not his personality. He never sought to socialise with Iago and, for that matter, neither did anyone else.

* * *

"Is there any truth behind it, or is it just a vicious rumour?" Helen, the secretary to both Caxton and Iago, asked. She was asking herself as much as anyone else.

"I wouldn't be surprised if it's just a rumour," said Gertrude.

"I wouldn't be surprised if it was Caxton playing away rather than his wife," Phaedra then suggested mischievously. "His Nibs seems to have a roving eye to me!"

Gertrude ignored the Features Editor's flippancy and asked Helen if she had heard the rumour from anyone other than Iago. "What *are* you getting at?" Helen responded in feigned amazement. "As if I didn't know!" Phaedra gave her a nudge to indicate that Iago was entering the room.

The Deputy Editor stood and gazed at everyone in the room before sauntering towards a shelf at the side that housed some recent editions. After a perfunctory read, he walked towards where Cicero sat, stood over him and asked: "Have you heard anything from Marcus yet?" Cicero replied that he had not, and Iago went over to Titus, who sat opposite to Gertrude. Helen and Phaedra had, by then, returned to their workstations.

"How's the election work going?" Iago asked Titus, who assured him that everything was under control. "Good!" Iago said crisply. "Any idea where Adonis is?" he then asked.

"At the Big Cheese Stadium, I believe," Titus replied. "I understand he's competing in the shot-put today." Iago nodded, turned and left the room.

* * *

Plenty of voters were at the 'Big Cheese' to watch Adonis and others compete in the annual Andronicus Athletics Championships. Many had travelled from out of town, having cast their votes en route or vowing to do so afterwards. Polling

Day also happened to be the first of the two-day sporting event. The first day was devoted to field events, such as the javelin, discus, hammer throwing, long jump, high jump, hop skip and leap, and tossing the tree trunk, as well as the shot-put. The second day would see a variety of track races and a marathon that would start and finish inside the stadium and run along a specially marked-out route in-between.

As expected, Adonis was victorious with the shot. His main rival, Boxer, was otherwise engaged, of course, and the only competitor to come even close to the putts Adonis accomplished turned out to be a young, unknown putter from the outskirts of Carthage.

The day was a particularly busy one for Adonis, who was responsible for covering the championships for the *Standard*, and in addition, he had to make sure to get his vote in for Caxton and be in the Town Hall at the end of the day when the election results would be announced.

Caxton arrived at the hall in good time. He had donned his best suit, adorned it with 'Vote for Caxton' regalia and, if that was not enough, had his beautiful wife Ophelia on his forearm. He was standing for Parliament for the first time, having decided to brush aside suggestions of a conflict of interest. "As a councillor, I will make sure that my readers will be better informed than ever," he had declared.

When the results were announced, there were a lot of cheers and no surprise. The Status Quo Party was victorious again but, as expected, with a slightly reduced majority. Caxton scraped home by the narrowest of margins. His most ardent supporters, including Adonis, gathered round to congratulate him and Caxton invited them to join him for celebrations at his home.

"I suppose you will have to offload a lot of your duties on to your deputy, now that you are a councillor," one supporter suggested.

"Don't worry about that," Caxton replied with one of his famous smiles. "We've got all that planned and sorted out." Then, under his breath, he added: "I do that, anyway!"

As always, Ophelia smiled demurely and said little during the proceedings. The fact that she kept her thoughts to herself added to her aura of mystery. It was an aura, which, coupled with beauty, brains and breeding, had had a devastating effect on male suitors before she met and married Caxton.

Before meeting Caxton, she had been wooed endlessly, mainly in the highest social circles, and was regarded as the island's top female catch. Ophelia, whose manners were impeccable and whose intellect was superior to that of nearly all her suitors, always let them down lightly. She never had a bad word to say about anyone, and all the failed courtships ended amicably. Then along came Caxton.

The handsome, charismatic journalist with a glittering future swept her off her feet. The courtship was brief, and the pair were married within months. The wedding, followed by a reception at the palatial home of Ophelia's parents on a rural estate twenty miles to the north of Phoenix, was one of the social events of the year. As expected, Ophelia was exquisitely dressed for the occasion and, while hardly uttering a word, was the main focus of attention.

The main topic of conversation among guests was how the silent, serene and seemingly imperturbable bride would fare in the future with such a loquacious, demonstrative and, at times, fiery groom. "I suppose it's a case of opposites attracting," some of the guests guessed, and the others just hoped they were right.

The couple set up home in a salubrious part of Phoenix that was within easy reach of the main *Standard* office and had two offspring. Ophelia showed herself to be a devoted wife and mother and socialised sparingly. She did, however, make a point of being by her husband's side when he needed to attend prestigious press events. The presence of a spouse, especially a beautiful one, was to Caxton's advantage on such occasions.

Caxton revelled in the role of a happy and successful family mouse. However, it was known that, before he met Ophelia, he had a roving eye and a predilection for playing harder than he worked. Ophelia never indicated an awareness of such a reputation, and the subject of celibacy or otherwise was never brought up in her presence.

As a married mouse, Caxton had been heard, more than once, to say: "Ophelia is my rock. She is the love of my life." One or two cynical observers – and there were plenty of cynics in the world of journalism – had suggested that the rock might be about to shift. There had been the occasional post-marital dalliance for Caxton, and there was speculation over what would happen if Ophelia found out.

If there was any hint of suspicion in Ophelia's mind, she did not show it. One possible reason was that she was receiving overtures herself. Whether or not they were welcome was unclear, though one young reporter at the *Standard* had told colleagues he had seen her in the embrace of a male far younger than herself.

CHAPTER 14

Polo had reached the top rung before he realised something was amiss. Rosencrantz and Boxer were standing well away from the hole, and they had no idea either. It was only when he heard a muffled scream from below and then saw an angry cloud of dust that seemed to envelop everything lower than the middle rung. The cloud, of a copper hue, hung in the same position for about thirty seconds before it settled slowly on top of Marcus and the massive book he had just closed.

"Pass me a water bottle!" Polo barked with an air of urgency that startled the other two. "And a large cloth!" Rosencrantz duly obliged. Polo poured some water on the cloth, which he then tied round his nose and mouth. On reaching Marcus, he lifted the latter's head up and poured some water into his mouth. Marcus opened his eyes and began to cough and convulse violently. Polo patted him hard on the back and did his best to ensure that he was in a safe breathing position.

Eventually, the convulsing and coughing stopped, and Polo asked Marcus if he was able to climb up the rungs that would take them out of the hole. Marcus tried to get up but fell back into a sitting position. "I feel terrible," he said. "I feel so weak! And all because of a cloud of dust!" Polo pointed out that this was no ordinary dust. He then called up to Boxer, asking him to join them. "I have never come across dust like this before," he added. "One thing I do know is that you're going to need some time to recuperate."

As soon as Boxer had carried Marcus to the top and put him down in the most comfortable position possible, Polo said: "I'm going to go ahead on my own to see if there is a decent resting place somewhere." He instructed Rosencrantz and Boxer to keep an eye on Marcus and give more water, if necessary. "If something really bad happens, use your whistles," he added.

Not long after Polo had gone, Marcus began to perk up a bit. Rosencrantz passed a water bottle to him and asked him how he felt. "Much better than I was a few minutes ago," Marcus replied. "The pain has gone, and I thought for a time that I had gone blind. The pain was everywhere, from top to bottom, and especially in the eyes and inside my head. And I couldn't breathe. I thought my lungs were going to burst! I still feel a bit strange now."

Rosencrantz asked in what way.

"I feel as if I have been… violated!" Marcus said. "I feel as if the dust – and I can't help wondering if it really was dust, or something else – got into every part of my body. It got into my eyes, mouth, throat, ears, bloodstream, everywhere. I even get the feeling that it has taken over my mind!"

Rosencrantz looked nonplussed and Boxer baffled. "How can dust do all that?" the latter asked.

"I wish I knew," Marcus replied. "All I know is that I have never, ever, come across anything like it before. But if it wasn't dust, what else could it be?"

Just under an hour later, Polo returned with the news that he thought he had found somewhere suitable to go to. "It's going to be a bit tricky getting there and we will be needing Boxer's muscles again," he said. Polo asked Marcus how he felt now and, when the latter declared himself fit to move, Rosencrantz helped him to get up and Boxer took charge of his rucksack.

The next part of the journey was straightforward at first. The going underfoot was even and easy, with the quartet walking in single file. Marcus experienced a little shortness of breath at first and was obliged to slow down slightly, but his strength and resolve returned quickly, and within minutes, he was able to proceed at his normal pace.

When the quartet reached the tricky part that Polo had referred to, they were presented with two options. One was to go straight ahead, the other to go sharply to the right. The tunnel ahead was narrower, with less head room, and seemed to get warmer with every step taken along it. It felt decidedly claustrophobic, too. The turning to the right offered more space and went downwards. It did, however, entail tackling a sharp descent.

"I think it's pretty clear which way we must go," Polo announced. Without waiting for a response, he turned and led the others to a point where the quartet would have to scramble downwards. "All right, Marcus?" he asked. The latter went puce but nodded.

"Don't worry," Polo told him. "We will tie a rope round you and keep an eye on you as we go down."

After a short rest, the descent began. Despite the fact that it was longer than expected, with visibility gradually worsening, Marcus coped surprisingly well. His new lease of life was so apparent that even Polo was taken aback. The quartet progressed slowly but reasonably surely, with a mixture of walking, sliding and scrambling. As they descended, they discovered that the width of the downwards slope was variable. Sometimes, it was possible to travel down four abreast. At others, it had to be one at a time.

At one point, a gaping hole appeared above them on the left, and it was possible to see the peak of a volcano… probably the same as the one seen before.

A little further down, the quartet reached an area that was flat, smooth and square and almost resembled a first-floor landing of a large house. To the extreme right was a long flight of steps that ran sharply downwards. The steps were a grimy grey and had bits of mould on them. There were walls on either side and these, too, were grey with traces of mould. The steps and walls had a suggestion of dampness about them, too. More importantly, they conjured up memories of the visit to the Rats' Palace.

As they made their way down the steps, they could hear the sound of running water. The sound became louder with every step. After a while, there was a slight turning to the right, and a large pool with a path to one side could be seen. Once on the path, they could see they were close to the entrance of a cave and that the cave was behind a waterfall. The path took them to the side of and beyond the waterfall and on to the edge of a lake.

The lake was surrounded on all sides by towering cliffs. The only gap of any size in the cliffs was the space from which the waterfall could cascade from the top and deposit the contents of a river into the lake. The cliffs jutted outwards at the top. At the far end of the lake was a small opening which allowed excess water to be filtered away. The water that remained in the lake was so clean that the travellers could see their reflections in it. Unfortunately, the path only allowed them to walk a short way along one side before ending abruptly.

They all craned their necks in an attempt to assess the height of the cliffs. "I would say between four and five hundred feet," said Polo. "One thing's for sure: we're almost totally enclosed."

Marcus added: "We seem to be in a sort of cocoon, a haven of safety from all the island's ills. And, come to think of it, it's a bit like a prison as well… though a very attractive one!"

Rosencrantz then pinpointed a practical problem. "At some point, we're going to have to travel on the lake, and we have got only one dinghy that will take just two of us at a time."

Polo responded by instructing him to get the dinghy out from the luggage and get it inflated. "Time to have a recce," he said.

The task of inflating the dinghy inevitably fell on Boxer, who completed it with just a few breaths and asked who would be getting on board. "It had better be me on my own, to start with," said Polo. "The rest of you can keep an eye open for anything interesting that might crop up."

At that very moment, a ripple appeared in the water about ten yards away and Rosencrantz said he thought that, for a split second, he saw a tiny head appear above the surface and then disappear. "It looked like the head of a water vole," he said. "But they don't exist anymore… do they?!"

Rosencrantz was known for his reliability and common sense, and the others accepted that he was unlikely to succumb to hallucinations. "We must keep our eyes peeled," Polo said matter-of-factly as he set up the dinghy. The others watched him set off, approach the gap at the end and disappear through it. They also looked for signs of life but saw none.

Marcus, Rosencrantz and Boxer had a long wait ahead of them. As the minutes and then the hours rolled by, Marcus looked at the gerbil and the hamster and observed that neither was in the least bit concerned. Rosencrantz reassured him that their leader knew what he was doing, and Boxer pointed out that they had both travelled with him many times before. Eventually, the dinghy reappeared and, as it drew nearer, a triumphant smile could be seen on Polo's face. "You will have to be ferried one at a time," Polo announced, once he was well within earshot.

Getting the group to where they were going entailed four separate outings, with one rodent rowing with the one oar they possessed, and the other as a passenger and guide, and one one-way trip involving transporting the baggage. Boxer took over the oar for the last two trips, leaving the others to take a good look at their new surroundings with the aid of torches.

What they saw was a narrow stream with a path running along one side of a tunnel. The ceiling was low, which meant stooping in some places for a six-footer. About fifty yards along the path, a hole could be seen a couple of feet up. The hole provided access to a small cave, which led to a much bigger cave. The latter was full of stalagmites and stalactites, and the sound of dripping water could be heard from one corner. The temperature had dropped by several degrees, and a feeling of dampness could be felt in the bones.

Polo and Marcus sat with the baggage while Boxer rowed back to pick up Rosencrantz. While they waited, they heard the sound of something moving in the water and, when a torch was trained on to the spot concerned, they could see a ripple. A little later, they spotted another ripple and, a while after that, suspected that they heard the sounds of tiny pattering feet coming from the big cave. "Let's stay where we are until the others join us," Marcus suggested.

Before Polo could reply, the dinghy had returned. Polo whispered to the other two that they could be in unexpected company. Four torches were then used to shed more light on their surroundings. Two tiny footprints could now be seen on the damp and grimy floor of the smaller cave, which was no more spacious than an average double bedroom.

The bigger cave turned out to be massive, far more so than it first appeared to be. There were stalagmites and stalactites everywhere, making it almost impossible to move around without bumping into one. The quartet shone their torches all around and could see that the inside of the cave was about twenty feet high in places and almost as spacious as a sports pitch. At one point, they thought they heard the sound of voices above the drip-drip-dripping of water coming down from a topmost corner.

The quartet moved closer to the centre of the cave. They could see that the stalagmites and stalactites often almost touched each other. Rosencrantz suddenly called out, "Hey!" Polo asked what was up. "I have just seen a pair of tiny eyes!" he was told. "They were over there," Rosencrantz said, pointing to one of the stalagmites.

"I see some eyes, too," said Boxer, pointing in a different direction.

"So can I," said Marcus. The quartet looked all around them and saw different pairs of eyes peering at them from all directions. It suddenly dawned on them that they were surrounded.

"Hello!" Polo called out. "Is anyone there?" In the absence of a response, he repeated the question and did so several times until the pattering of tiny feet and whispers could be heard. Some of the pairs of eyes then disappeared.

A moment later, a small outline, half hidden by a stalagmite, could be seen halfway up a wall and directly ahead but some distance away. "What is it you want?" the outline asked, in a surprisingly deep voice.

"We come in peace," said Polo. All the quartet could see was the outline, plus a pair of boring eyes and other eyes elsewhere. "We are not here to cause trouble. We are just friendly travellers," Polo added.

"Why are you here? What do you expect from us?"

"We are explorers. We do not expect anything. We want to know more about the Isle of Andronicus and who lives on it. Nothing more."

"Where have you come from?"

"From the town of Phoenix on another part of the island."

The outline could be heard exchanging whispers with another, smaller outline that had just emerged beside the first one. "Phoenix is a big place, isn't it?" the bigger outline asked.

"That's right," said Polo. "As far as we know, it has the biggest population of anywhere on the island." The smaller outline disappeared.

"You have come a long way," the bigger outline observed in a tone that was softer than before and sounded less suspicious. "And you have come all this way just to see what the island is like?" The tone was now laced with incredulity.

Marcus decided to contribute to the dialogue. "We did embark on this expedition to look for gold as well, and we are also hoping to learn more about the origins of mousekind," he said.

The outline moved and stood in front of the stalagmite he had been hiding behind. The travellers could now see they were talking to a male water vole, a species of rodent that the quartet had only seen previously in school textbooks. Standing on his hind legs, he was just over three feet tall, distinguished-looking and possessing the bearing of both a leader and a sage.

"Have you found any gold?" the water vole asked.

"Yes, we did," said Polo. "We can tell you where you can find it and you can even have some of the gold we picked up and put in our baggage. You are welcome to have some of our food, too."

The vole moved forwards a little more, and the travellers were able to see a hint of a smile.

"My name is Neptune," the vole said. "Please forgive the chilly reception, but I needed to be sure you were really what you said you were and that you really were here in peace. We had good reason to believe that you might not be."

Polo introduced himself and the others, and Marcus then said: "It sounds as if you are no stranger to trouble."

"That's an understatement!" the vole said. "As a breed, we have been harassed and persecuted for generations. There was a time when water voles could be seen all over the island. My late uncle, Hermes, who, in his time, was renowned for his wisdom and intellect, told me this. However, we have fallen prey to other rodents – mainly mice, I am afraid to say – and almost wiped out. A massive pandemic played a part in this, too." Neptune paused, seemingly to ensure that his visitors had understood the magnitude of what he had told them.

"Is this why you are in this out-of-the-way place now?" Marcus asked.

Neptune nodded. "I can see we have a mouse with intellect among us!" he answered. "If you had been born earlier – who knows – you might have kept the persecutors in check and made them see the folly of their ways!"

"So, why are you in this place in particular?" The question this time came from Rosencrantz, who had been dying to chip in.

"And I can see you are intelligent, too… for a gerbil!" Neptune offered a deep-throated chuckle. "This is our safe haven!" he boomed. "No one has been able to find us, until you came along.

"This is partly because we have been protected by a volcano. You must have seen it on your travels. Up until now, no being has dared to go near it, for fear of incurring its wrath. However, the volcano seems to have lost some of its potency in recent years. There was a time when it tossed out lava with such ferocity and at such regular intervals that anything anywhere near it risked being burned to a crisp. Now it throws up intermittent embers."

The visitors were enthralled. "So, how did you get to this haven in the first place?" Polo asked.

Neptune gave a deep sigh. "That was many generations ago," he said. "All I can tell you, from information passed down to me by Hermes and others, is that there was a mass escape. Most of the persecutors, as I have already said, were mice. The escape was planned well in advance and involved literally thousands of voles from all over the island. They chose a time when they thought the volcano would be at its least active and came this way under cover of darkness. The volcano erupted and at least two thirds of the escapees perished in a path of lava."

"That's both terrible and incredible!" exclaimed Marcus. "The escapees must have been very brave, as well as desperate."

"They were certainly desperate!" Neptune agreed.

"What exactly were they escaping from? And how many voles actually made it here?"

Neptune stepped backwards, and the smaller of the two outlines seen earlier could now be seen sidling up to him. The pair began to whisper to each other and disappeared. The whispering went on for a long time and had an air of urgency about it. At one point, it even sounded frantic. The quartet could also hear whispers from other parts of the cave.

At long last, Neptune came back into view. The smile was now gone. "You ask many questions," he said. "We are not interested in your gold, and we would like you to go back the way you came."

"What have we done wrong?" asked Polo.

"What was wrong with the questions?" asked Marcus. "We are only trying to be friendly."

"I am sorry," Neptune said politely but firmly. "My companions, or should I say the rest of my family, are becoming nervous, and they are my first concern."

"We are sorry, too, if we have made you feel uncomfortable in some way," said Polo. "We shall, of course, accede to your wishes and be on our way."

However, before any decision could be made on exactly what way that would be, Neptune said: "Before you go, there are two things I could tell you, though not much. Are you interested?"

"Yes, very much so," said Polo.

"There was a time when the island was ruled by a completely different species," said Neptune. "I don't know what species, only that they were not voles, mice or any other kind of rodent. Then, one day, something happened, and they were all wiped out. They became extinct. I do not know the cause, though one theory is that there was a highly infectious plague that killed everything off, apart from rodents. A series of battles for power followed, and the mice came out on top. The mouse leader at that time ruled that, in order to cement mouse power, all other rodents should be exterminated. The campaign of mass killings almost succeeded and would have done had not a less tyrannical leader taken over and put an end to the cull."

The quartet needed time to take that in. Eventually, Marcus managed to say: "I must admit, I have never seen a live vole before today, apart from in school textbooks."

"Mind you," said Neptune, "there are precious few of us left now. We are down to just a dozen. Diseases have taken their toll over the years, as well as the volcano and the occasional battle with rats or shrews... which I believe are extinct now."

Polo thanked Neptune for his help, and the quartet, still unsure of where to go, began to depart.

"Your best bet might be to go towards the volcano," said Neptune, who had been reading their thoughts. "The little river you have been on will get smaller going the other way, and you will end up at a hole that's even too small for an ant to get through!"

"But isn't the volcano dangerous?" Marcus asked.

"Yes, it is, but much less so than it used to be. If you go right inside it, you will find a tunnel that will give you a shortcut back to at least part of the way you came. I have only seen the path once myself, but I remember Hermes telling me many years ago how useful it could be."

Polo thanked Neptune again, and the latter replied: "Good luck. You are not likely to see us again. Now that the volcano is losing some of its power, we might well feel obliged to move on ourselves."

CHAPTER 15

There was nothing for it for the quartet but to retrace their steps for the moment. A decision could be made later on the question of whether to follow Neptune's advice to the letter and go home via the volcano or seek new fields to conquer. The case for heading homewards looked strong. They had covered a substantial part of the island, they had found gold and had unearthed some documents that needed to be deciphered. For Polo, the challenge of The Oven remained as 'unfinished business', but all in all, there was plenty to report.

Marcus was convinced that the documents held the key to much of what they had been seeking to learn and favoured getting back home as soon as possible so he could take steps to establish the truth. Polo, on the other foot, wanted to see everything there was to see. To miss something was, in his eyes, a failure. His inability to penetrate The Oven was something that seriously rankled.

The process of getting back to where they had first launched the dinghy was lengthy and tedious. Once all the toing and froing had been done, Polo made an announcement: "We are going back to the volcano. We will locate the tunnel that Neptune told us about first, but I also want to look out for routes that might take us elsewhere."

Marcus knew that the last part of his decision was wrong. He did not know why; he just knew. His self-confidence and assertiveness had grown during the last few days. So, too, had his intuitiveness. It was as if there was something new coursing through his veins, and feelings of fear in particular had been almost totally suppressed.

However, he was well aware of Polo's renown as an explorer and a leader who rarely, if ever, made a mistake. He knew, too, that Rosencrantz and Boxer were both totally loyal to their leader and would never challenge or even question any decision he made... and would undoubtedly side with Polo in the event of any sort of argument. So, for the moment, Marcus kept his counsel.

Marcus's time was to come later when fate played a hand. It happened just before the quartet reached the foot of the volcano. The air had become almost unbearably hot and the smoke that filled it made breathing difficult and progress slow. Any vegetation that remained was burning and the ground was littered with red lumps that were difficult to avoid.

Disaster struck when the normally sure-footed Polo stepped into a hidden hole and turned an ankle as he fell. At almost exactly the same time, an acrid plume of smoke from an ultra-large ember flew into his face and blinded him. Polo screamed in agony, before gathering his senses. "I can't walk and I can't see," he told the others. "You are going to have to help me."

Rosencrantz showed, as he had done many times before, how resourceful he could be. After rummaging feverishly in the largest rucksack, he fished out two long pieces of wood, four small metallic wheels, a hammer, a chisel and a box of nails and, in just over an hour, managed to create a sledge-cum-buggy that Polo could sit or lie on. He then produced a length of rope, which could be used to stop him falling off.

Marcus congratulated Rosencrantz on his handiwork, before referring to the need to 'find that tunnel', and no one argued. "The decision is out of my paws," said Polo, who did his best to mask the pain he was in. "I'm no use to anyone at the moment, and I will go along with whatever the rest of you say." Marcus was about to say that perhaps it was time to go home but did not need to when Polo suggested that himself!

"I'll go and look for where the tunnel is," Marcus said. Without waiting for a response, he shot up what passed for a path and left Rosencrantz and Boxer gaping in amazement at his newly found audacity. Marcus instinctively knew where the tunnel was, and it was not long before he could signal success with a wave to the others.

The tunnel was, in fact, only about fifty feet up, but the route to it was steep and rocky, and Marcus needed to go down to help with the task of carrying Polo. "I didn't know you were so strong!" exclaimed Boxer, who, once again, was amazed.

The tunnel was by no means easy to locate, and Marcus's ability to spot it so quickly was yet another source of surprise. It was accessed via a number of tiny mountainside openings. Most of the openings led to nowhere. The one Marcus found was half-hidden by a piece of rock that jutted across it, and there was room for just one rodent to squeeze through at a time.

The tunnel itself was dark and narrow, making it a tight squeeze for Polo and the contraption carrying him. Polo had had to get off the contraption to get through the hole. However, it did at least provide plenty of headroom, a smooth path to walk on and surprisingly clean air. The journey along it seemed to last forever, though. Marcus somehow knew that it would take the quartet to where they wanted to go, and he was able to instil that feeling of confidence into the others.

The other good news was that, after a day, Polo announced that he was feeling a lot better. "I'm starting to see things again, and I reckon I'll be able to walk again soon," he said.

After two more days, Polo was back on his feet and his sight was almost fully restored. But he remained content to let Marcus remain in charge, for the time being at least, as he recognised his qualities as a leader. The way Marcus had changed during the course of the expedition, especially after his discovery of the scrolls, was a revelation. Not only had his self-confidence and physical strength grown out of all recognition, but he had also developed an explorer's nose, a sixth sense. He had learned where to go, what to do and how to react in situations in many ways for which there was no blueprint. He could think outside the box.

Polo had had dealings with other explorers for much of his life and knew that much could be learned from studying textbooks, practical experience and sheer hard graft. However, there were some qualities, such as powers of intuition and an ability to address a problem for which there was no obvious answer, that could not be taught. Polo could see these qualities in Marcus, even though he was still a tyro.

Marcus managed to keep the others in an upbeat frame of mind as the expedition continued for hour after hour, day after day. The quartet ate and slept when necessary on the tunnel floor. The food supply began to run low, as did the torch batteries which needed to be replaced soon. At times, the tunnel path went upwards, downwards, to the left and to the right. And, at the front of everyone's mind was the fact that the Temperate Season was due to end soon and give way to the Cold Season. Marcus was under the impression that season changes in some parts of the island might be less pronounced, but he was in no doubt as to what would lie in wait in and around Phoenix.

The end of the trek along the tunnel was abrupt. It was heralded by a ray of sunlight that shone through an overhead opening. The tunnel itself shrank and became impassable. So, the quartet squeezed through the opening after widening it to make room for Boxer.

They found themselves on a path halfway up the side of a mountain. Marcus looked upwards, downwards, across a ravine and to the left and right and, without a word, began to walk to the right. The others were taken aback by the absence of consultation but were too weary to argue. Even Polo did not demur.

After a couple of hours, the terrain looked familiar, and Marcus identified it as an early part of the approach to the Rats' Palace. "The Cold Season is about to begin, and we must head homewards without delay," he said. "The chances are that we won't be able to make it before the blizzards begin, and we will probably have to seek refuge in Carthage."

CHAPTER 16

A buzz of excitement could be heard throughout the underground rooms of the *Phoenix Standard*. The Cold Season had arrived, the staff had had to move hurriedly, and another significant story was breaking. The news that Da Vinci had managed to create a Flying Machine had reached the *Standard* two weeks ago… and just one day before the building above ground had to be vacated.

"Marcus is back!" the Chief Reporter's secretary Gertrude announced to everyone within earshot. "He's in Carthage." Titus, who had been directing reporters to produce the best possible coverage relating to Da Vinci's latest invention, looked up instantly.

"I want to talk to him urgently!" he said. Gertrude told her boss that Marcus had set foot in Carthage less than an hour ago, was exhausted, needed to rest first and would be in touch shortly.

Titus rose onto his hindfeet, left the underground newsroom and went to see Iago, who was at the helm that day. The reporters looked towards Gertrude in the hope that she could tell them more. "I should imagine Marcus is absolutely shattered!" said Cicero.

"Undoubtedly!" Gertrude agreed. "It sounds as if the expedition was really gruelling. Polo got injured towards the end of it and, believe it or not, Marcus took over as leader. They are now all resting up in accommodation laid on by the Mayor of Carthage."

"Did you say Marcus became the *leader*?!" the youngest reporter asked. His tone of incredulity reflected the feeling of all those present.

"Yes, it looks that way," said Gertrude. "There's nothing else I can tell you just now, only that a council official was phoning on his behalf… and on his instructions."

At this point, Titus returned to the newsroom with an air of excitement and agitation that was even greater than usual. "We're going to have some really good stuff in the paper the next few weeks," he said. "First the Flying Machine… and now this!"

He turned to Cicero. "I want you to establish contact with Marcus as soon as you can and make sure we have a good series of reports on the expedition itself and some tip-top interviews as well. I would also like you to talk to Polo and the other two who took part in the expedition. We can have 'personality profiles' on all four of them. Phaedra can oversee the whole project, and she can also lend a paw with the writing. And I will get one of the reporters to provide input if needed."

Cicero had the good sense not to telephone Marcus too soon. Gertrude had provided him with contact details, and although the clear message was for him to proceed without delay, he decided that the best course of action was to collate some background information before disturbing his colleague.

Phaedra, meanwhile, was busy trying to extract as much information as she could from the elusive and, at times, uncommunicative Da Vinci. Although she was in overall charge of the expedition coverage, she was unlikely to have time to be involved in it for a while. However, Cicero was experienced enough as a journalist and at handling rodents generally to know that being overzealous could be counterproductive. So, he took his time.

He had the ability to read situations better than most and could read Marcus better than any mouse alive. He knew Marcus and the others would need at least two days before having to field questions. And he was less surprised than anyone else that Marcus had shown he had it in him to take over as leader.

Cicero had been spot on with his prediction that the expedition would be gruelling and, at times, life-threatening. What he was not aware of was Marcus's powers of intuition, without which the entire project might have foundered. This particularly applied to the last part when the weather conditions were appalling and an intimate knowledge – or pure luck – was needed.

Marcus, whose experience of exploring had previously been limited to a walk through hills that surrounded Troy, had taken over as leader and, inexplicably, knew exactly where to go when he did. The wind was whistling and biting, the driven snow blinding and visibility often limited to a few paces ahead. The peaks, paths, mountain edges and crevices all looked the same. Yet, Marcus was able to lead the others to safety. Even Polo was amazed at his ability to find the right paths, the right places to find shelter and even the right times to take it. The chill wind cut into every layer of clothing and tested the toughest constitutions. So, it was hardly surprising that the travellers were in a state of collapse when they reached Carthage.

When Cicero did eventually get in touch with Marcus, the latter was delighted to hear that he was the one chosen to handle the expedition coverage. Cicero promised to arrange for a snow bus to collect Marcus and the three others as soon as weather conditions looked likely to ease a bit. "That's very kind of you, but there's no rush!" said a jubilant-sounding Marcus. "The Carthaginians are spoiling us something rotten!"

* * *

Phaedra, meanwhile, was being put to the test in a different way. At long last, she had managed to track down Da Vinci and persuade him to grant her an interview. She had met him briefly twice before and looked forward to their third encounter with some trepidation. The Features Editor was known for her vivacity, persistence, self-assurance and, when necessary, forcefulness. She had never been accused of reticence or of being a shrinking violet, and yet she found the iconic inventor intimidating.

Da Vinci had rented a massive workshop in the remotest part of underground Phoenix and had arranged for all his goods and equipment to be transported there a week before the end of the Temperate Season. The workshop was at the end of a road on the underground settlement's periphery. It was part of an estate of small factories, garages, waste disposal plants, warehouses and other, smaller workshops. However, Da Vinci's workshop stood alone, and any activity that took place in it could be kept secret.

The journeys from both the *Standard* office and Phaedra's underground home were from different directions, and both entailed negotiating roads that could sometimes be winding and circuitous and, at others, heavily laden with traffic. The estate where Da Vinci's workshop was housed had an eerie, deserted and forbidding feel about it. It even gave the impression of being cut off from the rest of Phoenix. The workshop itself was guarded by a giant iron gate that had been bolted shut at the top and bottom. To one side was a small, metal door with a keyhole but no knocker or handle. Phaedra gave the door a rat-tat-tat with her powder compact.

The door opened and Da Vinci appeared. He was clad in overalls. A perfunctory head movement indicated that she could enter. "Mind the step," Da Vinci said in his surprisingly high-pitched voice. Phaedra stepped down onto a stone floor. Most of the workshop was dimly lit, but in the centre, a bright light beamed down on to a tarpaulin-covered contraption that was, presumably, Da Vinci's latest invention. About ten paces to one side of the invention was a table with chairs either side, and Da Vinci invited Phaedra to sit.

Da Vinci gazed at his guest for a moment with a pair of eyes that could have been designed to terrorise. The eyes were dark, piercing and had red flecks round the edges. The redness was reputed to be accentuated in moments of anger. Although elderly and in physical decline, he was still an imposing figure at over six feet tall, with a sturdy build, muscular gait and a scar down one side of his face.

"I will talk to you about the Flying Machine and about my work generally but not about my private life," he said firmly. His reputation for not wasting words was well established.

"Thank you for seeing me," Phaedra responded in a tone that matched his. "The reason I am here is to talk about your latest project. From what I have heard, it could revolutionise the way we all live," she said.

Da Vinci offered Phaedra a rare smile before rising onto his hindfeet and tugging at the rope that held the tarpaulin over his latest brainchild in place. Phaedra saw a large metallic box that was slightly more spacious than the front cabin of a lorry. There were wheels beneath the box and, above it, a steel mast supporting two massive blades that resembled the type seen on windmills. The box had windows at the sides and, after craning her neck, Phaedra could see that it contained four seats... two at the front and two behind them.

"There you are!" said Da Vinci. "This is my latest baby... the Flying Machine! Apart from a tweak or two here and there, it's just about ready to go!"

"Wow!"

Da Vinci pointed upwards. "Do you see the blades at the top? They are the key to it. The machine includes a device that makes the blades go round, and when the blades are spinning really quickly, the whole machine will leave the ground and go straight upwards. Once it's up in the air, it can be steered in any direction."

Da Vinci then went back to the table, picked up a pile of papers held together by a bulldog clip and threw the papers towards Phaedra. "You can take this bundle away with you," he said. "It should tell you any technical stuff you need to know, including the various stages of development, and it should also give you an idea of how much time I have spent on it."

"How long ago did you start working on it?" Phaedra asked.

"I have been at it, on and off, for about five years… the precise details are in your possession."

"When do you plan to go up in the Flying Machine?"

"As soon as the weather conditions permit it."

"Where will you fly to?"

"The first flight will just be a local test flight, though in the long-term, I want to take the machine on bigger journeys, journeys that can be completed much more quickly than hitherto."

"Will you be using the machine to explore parts of the island we don't know?"

"That's very much at the back of my mind, though I am probably too old to undertake such a mission. I will probably have to show someone like Polo how to fly the machine and then get him to do it."

"Would The Oven be on your list of places to go to?" Phaedra had a feeling that this was probably the last question she could get away with asking just now.

Da Vinci's eyes glinted and the red flecks round the edges grew larger. "Watch this space!" the great inventor said coolly. Then he grinned, before walking with Phaedra to the small, metal door and thanking her for taking the trouble to see him.

Another of Da Vinci's more recent inventions was the Snow Bus. Created just over a year ago and designed to withstand the harshest of weather conditions and the toughest of terrain, it could accommodate up to a dozen passengers. Its most notable features were two sets of four wheels and two blades capable of negotiating ice beneath the bus. The wheels were taller than the bus itself, and the wheels and blades were all retractable. The bodywork, incorporating reinforced glass windows, had been designed to cut out the cold. However, a heating and ventilation system had been included just in case.

The Snow Bus had been on just three outings to date, but a glowing future for it had been predicted. So much so that a second bus, a twenty-seater, was in the pipeline.

Phaedra, who had attended the first bus's launch and its subsequent maiden trip to Troy and its surrounds, was keen to be the one to meet Marcus and the other explorers in Carthage. However, there was that tricky interview with Da Vinci to write up, not to mention paperwork to study. Da Vinci was, of course, a mouse with enormous influence and Phaedra needed to think carefully about the best way to proceed next. So, she reluctantly conceded that Cicero was the right mouse for the mission.

The erudite Cicero's feelings about the trip were ambivalent. The normally unremittingly ferocious blizzards were less severe than usual, and at times, there were no blizzards at all. The bus was driven by a burly but monosyllabic hamster, whose only skill in life could be found behind a wheel. The only other passengers were four rowdy gerbils who had overstayed their welcome while partying with friends in Phoenix. Unfortunately for Cicero, the party continued on the Snow Bus with heavy drinking, a blaring transistor radio, dancing and empty cans being hurled around. Eventually, the driver stopped the bus and told the revellers to shut up or get out. By then, the journey was almost four fifths completed and had left Cicero with palpitations and a state of decidedly ill humour.

The driving had been impeccable, though, and the monosyllabic hamster tackled the tricky conditions with aplomb. On arriving at Carthage, he took the bus to the central market square and parked it in a covered area near the town hall. The customary blizzard had become a zephyr, and a reception committee clad in buttoned-up overcoats and balaclava helmets was waiting. The committee was about twenty strong, with Marcus at the forefront and everyone smiling.

The revelling gerbils perked up again and acted as if they thought they were the ones being welcomed. The driver told them to clear off and, in so doing, uttered more words than he usually did in a week. Cicero was treated differently, though all he wanted to do was lie down somewhere.

CHAPTER 17

A sumptuous meal – followed by music, dancing, cabaret and speeches – was laid on at the town hall the same evening. Cicero, Marcus and the other explorers sat with the town mayor at the top table. Polo was, of course, the main guest of honour. It was highly unusual, almost unheard of, for a gerbil or hamster to receive top-table treatment, but, on this occasion, Rosencrantz and Boxer were considered to be more than deserving. In fact, even the Snow Bus driver had been given a place at another table and offered overnight accommodation at a respected bed and breakfast establishment nearby.

Conversation was convivial, with the mayor and his wife holding forth on matters pertaining to Carthage, as well as asking intermittent questions to Polo about the expedition: Cicero was seated beside the Editor of the *Carthage Journal*. Marcus sat opposite to Cicero, and the pair conversed when they could. "I want to show you some scrolls that we found," Marcus said early on. But serious talk was stifled by nearby jocularity, and Cicero was unable to take in much, anyway.

While refreshments consisting of wheat juice mixed with the best melted cheese were being served, the mayor rose onto his hindfeet and paid tribute to the 'intrepid' Polo and his 'heroic' team. He talked a little about local matters, too, before two other local dignitaries got up and expanded on these. The mayor then invited Polo to say a few words.

There were tumultuous cheers. The chance to get a glimpse of, and perhaps even meet, the fabled explorer was for many the main event and the only reason they were there at all. Polo, who was still feeling the effects of the rigours of the expedition, and his fall in particular, had been subdued that evening. However, he managed to talk succinctly about his latest venture and paid tribute to those who had accompanied him. He made special mention of Marcus.

"I could not have done it on my own," he told his fellow diners. "The other three each had a special part to play, and they were each essential to the venture's success. The biggest revelation, though, was Marcus, who had joined the expedition as an observer and whose role was to write about it. He joined us with no experience of exploration whatsoever, and the rest of us expected to have to carry him… possibly literally!"

Polo went on to describe Marcus's contribution, especially after the fall, and how he took over as leader. "I'm beginning to get a bit long in the tooth for this game and I have, for some time, been on the lookout for someone capable of helping me lead… and even taking over on occasions while I focus on planning. I never, in my wildest dreams, thought a total beginner could fill such a role. But to say I was wrong—"

Polo's flow was suddenly interrupted by the sound of a groan and an overturning chair. A steward, who had been standing near the back of the hall, ran up to where a prostrate form could be seen. It was Cicero. "Are you all right, Sir?"

the steward asked. Marcus repeated the question with greater urgency before a flustered mayor told the steward to telephone for an ambulance.

Marcus decided to accompany the semi-conscious Cicero to the town hospital, which was just under an hour's drive away, and spend the night at or near the patient's bedside. This, of course, meant foregoing the rest of the celebrations, which continued until the small hours. His actions were mainly driven by concern for his colleague. There was a second reason, however: he wanted to talk to Cicero in confidence and away from crowds.

Unfortunately, Cicero was in no fit state to talk coherently, and it became apparent that he would have to stay in hospital for some time. He had had a heart attack, and tests were needed to gauge the severity. Under the circumstances, Marcus had little option but to rejoin Polo and the others and return to Phoenix.

He telephoned Phaedra from the town hall to tell her what had happened. A harassed-sounding Features Editor asked how long Cicero was likely to be out of action, and Marcus told her it was impossible to say yet.

Phaedra sighed and paused, before saying: "There's nothing for it. You are going to have to take responsibility for the expedition coverage. I will help when I can, of course, but I have other things on my plate just now and won't have much time to be involved."

"No problem!" Marcus answered. He was well used to superiors being reluctant to place trust in him but on this occasion, became irritated.

"Are you sure you can manage?" Phaedra asked. Her tone was patronising.

"Yes, of course I can! Why shouldn't I be able to manage?!" Marcus's tone was decidedly testy.

A clearly taken-aback Phaedra then said, after a few seconds: "All right, all right! I will leave you to it for now."

"There's just one other thing," Marcus said, as Phaedra was about to hang up.

"What's that?"

"I need to talk to Da Vinci. Could you let him know that?"

"Why? What for?"

"Just do it, will you!" Marcus said angrily. "Let's stop wasting time!"

"All right, all right!" Phaedra said again. Only one mouse could have been more surprised at the way he had spoken to her... and that was Marcus himself!

Unknown to Marcus, Polo had been standing nearby and had overheard much of the conversation. "You have grown remarkably forceful!" the great explorer observed, with a wink. "Anyone would think that something magical had got into your veins!"

* * *

Da Vinci was unusually welcoming when Marcus called on him. A visit to the giant underground workshop was Marcus's first port of call on returning to Phoenix and having a short rest. Phaedra had set the meeting up, and Da Vinci had heard about the expedition and a little about Marcus's part in it.

"Any friend of Polo's is a friend of mine!" Da Vinci said as he ushered him in. "What you did was quite an accomplishment."

Marcus – whose self-confidence had, by now, grown out of all recognition – had expected a warm reception. He replied that it had been an honour to be associated with Polo.

"Even so, what you did was quite something!" The normally formidable Da Vinci was on the verge of drooling. Marcus instinctively knew that now was the time to explain the purpose of his visit.

After a few more expressions of admiration, the great inventor said: "Anyway, I'm sure you're not here to listen to an old mouse's wittering! How can I help you? I will certainly help if I can."

Marcus opened a large zip-up bag he had been carrying and fished out the scrolls he had discovered on the expedition, along with photographs of pages in the giant book that had to be left behind. He unrolled one of the scrolls on the table close to the covered-up Flying Machine and drew Da Vinci's attention to the strange drawings that were accompanied by indecipherable writing.

"The drawings are interesting in themselves and, as you can see, some of them are of creatures that can stand on their hind legs but look nothing like rodents," he said. "The words, assuming they are words, might explain what they are. But they are so faint that, try as I may, I can't make out what they say."

"Have you shown them to anyone else?" Da Vinci asked.

"A couple of historians in Carthage had a look. They said they could be some sort of power figures of the distant past. They also tried to work out the words with a magnifying glass but to no avail. I was also hoping to show them to my colleague Cicero, who is a bit of a historian himself, but he fell ill, and I never got the chance."

"And you would like me to have a go?"

"Yes, I was wondering whether you might have a more powerful magnifier or perhaps some sort of powder that would make the writing legible."

Da Vinci gave his whiskers a pensive stroke, before saying: "Let me show you my latest baby while I have a think." He removed the tarpaulin that was covering the Flying Machine and, after observing Marcus's admiring gaze, asked: "How do you fancy going up in this?"

"Just say the word, and I'll be up for it!" Marcus replied. And he meant it.

Da Vinci stroked his whiskers again. "Tell you what, leave the scrolls and papers with me and I will see what I can do," he said.

CHAPTER 18

Rumours of an attempted coup had been buzzing round the newsroom for several weeks before Marcus's return. Caxton had spent much of his time away, ostensibly on parliamentary duties, and at the same time, there had been whispers about his wife.

Iago, in his own subtle way, had been making his presence felt more than ever. He was widely seen as Caxton's heir apparent. Deputies did not automatically move up if an editor left, though, and it was not unusual on a newspaper for a mouse from outside the organisation to take over the reins. It was also possible for existing members of staff to leapfrog over their superiors, and there were those who believed Phaedra and Adonis were poised for a joint takeover.

The Chairman of the Board had been popping in from time to time, as he always had done but less often, and there was an unusually large number of mice keen to impress. The Chairman had, of course, been fully aware of Caxton's absences.

The only certainty at that time was Caxton's feeling of insecurity. The charismatic Editor was shrewd enough to know that Iago would happily displace him, given the chance. Caxton's new political duties were often onerous, but these galvanised him, rather than the reverse, and in no way sapped his energy. The cause of his insecurity was the perceived infidelity of his wife, Ophelia.

Caxton had to know the truth. It had become such an obsession with him that matters pertaining to Parliament, the *Phoenix Standard* and the well-being of his family had almost become trivial. He was well aware of how having such a mindset could be damaging, and so, the cause of his big worry had to be tackled without delay.

Yet the only concrete fact, if it could be called that, was someone saying that Ophelia had been seen in the company of a younger male mouse. His wife was still always available to support him when he wanted her to be with him at public functions. Her shoulder was always there to be cried on when needed, which was admittedly not often, and she was always happy to lend an ear or offer advice. On the face of it, she was continuing to be the perfect wife and mother to their offspring. There had been a couple of occasions recently when Ophelia, showing no little concern, had asked Caxton if anything was wrong. Her usually self-confident husband found himself unable to say what had been gnawing at him.

Caxton decided there was nothing for it but to do some detective work. He considered hiring a 'private eye' but concluded that he wanted no one else to know about his problem. He also feared that he could end up making a fool of himself if the matter became public knowledge. So, he opted for going it alone.

The first step was to let Ophelia believe he had gone to work as normal and then keep watch from somewhere unseen. As Ophelia rarely, if ever, went out with him during the evening, this meant playing detective during the daytime and at the expense of other commitments.

Caxton and Ophelia's underground home was in an up-market locality known for its parks, trees, a brook and various water features. The brook, conceived and created by Da Vinci, flowed in from above ground and ended in a cave halfway down a cliff. Opposite the couple's home was a small grassy area with bushes and a bench. It was possible to sit on the bench, turn round on it and watch comings and goings from it.

Caxton was prepared to spend literally hours in such a position until hunger and soreness from being in the same position for so long took hold. The first two vigils came to nothing. During the first, Ophelia was seen going out to do some shopping and returning within half an hour. During the second, she did not go out at all. A neighbour taking a walk saw him, gave him a curious look and wished him, "Good morning."

He was on the point of giving up during his third vigil, when he saw Ophelia leave the house, get into their buggy and head off. A bicycle was on hand nearby, and Caxton did his best to follow discretely and, at the same time, keep up. His heart missed a beat when he saw the buggy turn into a road that led to the most notorious underground area in Phoenix. The area had no official name but was widely referred to as 'The Slum'.

The road, known simply as 'The Connector', was arrow-straight and its purpose was to get traffic in and out of 'The Slum' as quickly as possible. There was a cycle path to one side, and Caxton was athletic enough to peddle hard and not be left too far behind.

Shortly after entering the neighbourhood, The Connector ended abruptly at a wide turning area. As the turning area came into view, Caxton could see the buggy veer sharply to the left and go down a smaller road that curved to the right. The curved road provided access to stone paths and grassy lanes going off it either side and ended when it met a line of the backs of houses and outbuildings. An alley in the middle led to a dingy market square.

Around the sides of the square was a variety of shops with grimy glass fronts and a few run-down terraced houses, some of them obviously empty. In the square itself were around thirty stalls laden with cheese, oats, fruit and other food, or utility items such as electrical goods, ironmongery and spare parts for bicycles or buggies. The stalls were ranged round a seating area where the locals could catch up on the latest gossip.

Ophelia's buggy had been parked a few yards away from the alley entrance. Caxton looked for a spot where he could leave his bicycle without Ophelia seeing it and ended up leaving it locked up in a second alley that led to a play area.

The market was small but bustling and a regular focal point for bargain-hunters and gossipmongers. The stallholders were all gerbils or hamsters, as were most of the customers. Mice were something of a rarity. Ophelia, who was conspicuous wherever she went anyway, could be seen making her way through the throng and towards the seating area.

Caxton was a big, striking-looking mouse and tended to be conspicuous, too. However, he managed to position himself behind a tall, portly hamster who was heading in the same direction. Then, on reaching the seating area, he made use of a stall with a tiered line of old bicycles for sale or awaiting repair as a means of camouflage.

He could see Ophelia walking to the far side of the seating area towards a single chair, on which a young male mouse was sitting. The young male, who was gaunt-looking and of similar height to Ophelia, rose onto his hindfeet as she approached and the two embraced. The embrace appeared to be tender and lasted for several seconds before Ophelia kissed the male on one cheek. The pair moved to a small bench a few feet away and began to talk in earnest.

Caxton could now see that his rival in love, if that was what he was, was very young indeed and far from prepossessing. "How could he possibly be Ophelia's lover?" he asked himself. "He's far too young and gauche... not to mention ugly!" But if he was not a lover, what was his wife seeing him for? Why didn't he know anything about it? His marriage to Ophelia had, from the very outset, been underpinned by an understanding that there would be no secrets between them.

Ophelia and the mysterious young male remained locked in conversation for a good half hour before they rose from the bench and made their way towards a small shop to the far right. Ophelia had an arm round the youngster's shoulders as they walked towards the shop and entered.

The shopfront was tiny and partly boarded up. The words 'Model Makers' could be seen, though only just, above a narrow wooden door to one side. The door had been painted a curious blue-cum-turquoise, and the paint was now flaking and the wood showing signs of rot. The words above were orange, and the paint used for them had become so faint that Caxton had to move closer to the shopfront to read them. The part of the front that was not boarded was plate glass from top to bottom. The glass was grubby and cracked, and just behind it could be seen a table laden with wooden models of houses, cars, buggies and various animals. The models were intricate and elegant and looked out of place.

Caxton needed to almost press his face against the glass to see what lay further inside. He observed a long, linoleum-covered corridor floor that stretched so far back that its end was almost out of sight. To the sides were shelves with more models on some of them and a small counter halfway along to the right. Behind the counter was a small, wizened-looking female gerbil, who was conversing with Ophelia while the young male mouse nosed among the shelves. Ophelia and the gerbil appeared to know each other well.

Caxton craned his neck and pressed his face on the glass hard. The gerbil looked in his direction, and so, too, did Ophelia. The latter visibly trembled and jumped backwards before fleeing to the back of the shop and out of sight. She had lost all her renowned composure. The gerbil followed and Caxton entered, with his composure gone, too. Caxton heard the sound of sobbing behind a door at the corridor's end. He approached the door and tried to open it.

"Go away!" a rough, rasping voice, presumably belonging to the gerbil, greeted his failed attempt.

"What are you doing here?" Ophelia then asked in tearful tones.

"Go away!" the gerbil rasped again. "You're not wanted here!"

Caxton banged on the door countless times but to no avail. He heard his wife sobbing and saying: "It's no good – he will never understand!" The gerbil told him to go away again. The charismatic, normally self-possessed Newspaper Editor considered trying to break the door down but decided that would do more harm than good.

He had never felt so devastated in his life. He did not know what he had done wrong or what to do next. The thought of the beautiful but highly respectable Ophelia not being true to him was unbearable. There was nothing for it, it seemed, but to leave the shop, return to his bicycle, go home and consider how best to confront Ophelia when she got back… assuming she was going to.

However, as he went through the alley that had led him to the market square, he saw a tiny shop with the words 'Tipples' painted above the entrance. The shop was much the same size as the one he had left a few minutes ago, but that was where the similarity ended. The door, walls and windowpanes were in pristine condition. Inside was a bar with stools nearby, a carpeted floor and several well-polished tables with chairs around them. The style of the interior was neat and simple, with everything kept in apple-pie order.

Behind the bar were two short, portly hamsters, who Caxton guessed were a married couple. A group of four young gerbils were chatting gaily at one of the tables, while two middle-aged hamsters were perched on bar stools.

The couple behind the bar and the pair on the stools gave Caxton a speculative look as he walked their way. "How can we help?" the male behind the bar asked.

"I will have whatever tipple you recommend," Caxton replied. The couple behind the bar exchanged winks before the male hamster declared that they had 'just the thing'.

Caxton stared vacantly in front of him as the female disappeared through a door behind her and returned two minutes later with a tall, slim glass containing a dark green liquid that had a cherry floating on top. "This is our Top Tipples Special," she declared while placing the glass before him. "It is a mixture of oat, grape and apple juice, plus all sorts of other goodies that have been heated up and left to stand for an hour to allow all the different flavours to meld together in the right way."

Caxton, who cared little about what it was, mumbled his thanks and took his Top Tipple Special to a table in the furthest away corner. He took a sip and then another and paid no heed to the looks the hamsters on the bar stools were giving him. He began to feel dizzy… and the next thing he knew was that he was lying across the doorstep in front of his home.

After struggling onto his hindfeet, he fumbled through his pockets and discovered that his wallet, containing personal information as well as money, was missing. His keys were still there, though, and he was at least able to get inside. He then realised that two full days had passed since his trip to 'The Slum'. A copy of the *Standard*, with the day's date on it, had been left on the kitchen table and confirmed this.

Next to the newspaper was an envelope with his name on it. His heart sank as he opened it. The note inside, in Ophelia's impeccable handwriting, was terse and to the point.

'I have decided to go away for a while and have taken the youngsters with me,' the note said. 'I will try to explain recent events in due course, though I don't like the way you followed me. In the meantime, I need time to decide what to do with my life and whether or not I want you to be part of it. If I have caused you distress, I deeply regret it'. The note was signed 'O'.

The note offered no indication of where Ophelia might have gone to or for how long she was likely to be away, though

Caxton feared the worst when he discovered that virtually all her clothes and personal belongings had gone.

Still feeling queasy and with a splitting headache after his time at 'Tipples', Caxton sat brooding in a sitting room corner for the rest of the day and most of the next. A couple of telephone calls from the *Standard* were deflected with the words, "Leave it to Iago, or if he's not there, talk to Titus," as he tried to deal with his despair. Negativity was not normally in his nature, though, and as his head cleared, the answer to the question of what he should do next became clear.

* * *

"I had a feeling you'd be back!" the wizened old gerbil said to Caxton as he walked into 'Model Makers' once more. The tone was less than friendly, but at least it was not nakedly hostile like the last time. Yet, he was far from sure what he should say.

"I should imagine you're looking for some answers," the gerbil added.

"I certainly am," said Caxton. "I have so many questions that I don't know where to start!"

The gerbil's expression softened a little, and she invited him to follow her into a room behind the door he had previously thought of knocking down. The room was small and furnished with just a table and two chairs, and the gerbil invited Caxton to sit.

"My name is Desdemona," she said. "I know what your name is already, and I have heard a lot about you."

Caxton tried to sound casual by saying, "Not all bad, I hope!"

Desdemona shook her head. "Not at all, far from it," she replied. "But there are a lot of things you don't know about your wife, and she is afraid of how you would react if you found out."

Caxton winced. "You make me sound like an absolute ogre!" he exclaimed. "Whatever have I done to make her afraid of me?"

Desdemona offered a hint of a smile, before saying: "I should imagine the main thing you want to know is who the youngster you saw Ophelia with in the market square is. Am I right?" Caxton nodded. "His name is Percival," Desdemona told him. "He's the son of a close friend who died recently, and Ophelia has been taking an interest in his welfare."

Caxton was not satisfied. He sensed that Desdemona was holding something back. "A close friend, you say... just how close a friend to my wife was he?" He could see that his host was fidgeting in her chair, and he had been in the newspaper business long enough to know when he was not being told the whole truth. "There's a bit more to it than that, isn't there?" he said.

Desdemona's fidgeting became even more pronounced under his gaze. "Your wife has always been faithful to you, if that's what's worrying you," she said desperately. "There's no doubt in my mind that she's been true to her marriage vows."

Caxton was visibly relieved, though he did wonder how Desdemona could possibly know something like that. And he was sure that there was still something she had not told him. "That's wonderful to hear, of course," he said with a hint of irony, "though I have a funny feeling that there's a but, but, but!"

"All right!" Desdemona screamed. "Percival is Ophelia's

son! There you are, I have said it! Ophelia was seeing someone else long before she met you. Her lover was from a lower-class family and was also half mouse and half hamster. Ophelia used to meet him in secret because she was terrified of the prospect of bringing disgrace into her family. As you know, her parents and other relatives are highly respectable and very straight-laced."

"So, Percival is Ophelia's love child…"

"You're getting there!"

"OK, so how could Ophelia keep something like that a secret? And what happened to the lover?"

Desdemona looked as if she was about to burst into tears. "His name was Achilles," she said. "His parents were great friends of my late husband and mine. Now they are all gone! Achilles was killed in a traffic accident, not knowing anything about the pregnancy. Later on, and before the pregnancy became obvious, Ophelia told her parents she was going away on a study course near Carthage, and she arranged to have Percival adopted at birth."

"So, how did Percival find out who his real mother was?"

"I gather it was from some local busybody, a parent or someone who knew Percival at school. The couple who had been looking after Percival as their son for all those years were forced to admit that they were not his biological parents, and Percival, understandably, wanted to know the whole truth."

"And he obviously did!"

"Yes, he did so quite recently. He found out about me and my connection with Achilles. I contacted Ophelia, who, in turn, contacted Percival. Ophelia promised to keep in touch, which is especially important to Percival because his adoptive parents are now in failing health and likely to die soon."

Caxton stroked his whiskers in a state of bemusement and shook his head. He was close to tears himself. "I would never have believed Ophelia could have been mixed up in something like this if you hadn't told me!" he said.

"Perhaps you don't know your wife as well as you thought you did!" Desdemona said with an ironic chuckle. "Don't forget that she could have ended the pregnancy but chose not to and that she is now looking out for her newly found son while he has big worries on his plate. I think you're lucky to have her!"

"Yes, but do I have her? I don't even know where she is!" Caxton's head was spinning. He had never before felt so unsure of himself or so insecure. "I want things to be right between us," he added desperately.

"I'm afraid I can't help you with that," said Desdemona. "I can only suggest that you go home and have a good think about what you should do next."

Caxton rose onto his hindfeet and was all set to leave, when he remembered he had one more question: "On the subject of going home, do you know anything about how I got home after my first visit here?"

Desdemona looked astonished. "Good grief! You must have got well and truly blotto at 'Tipples' not to remember that!"

"So, it seems!" Caxton mumbled.

"You were taken home by one of your reporters," Desdemona told him. "I happened to see the pair of you coming out of 'Tipples', and he was propping you up. He lives quite close by and hasn't worked on your newspaper for very long."

"Do you know his name?"

"I don't, I'm afraid. I have only had one short conversation with him, though I have seen him around quite a bit. He looks pretty young; I can tell you that."

"Did he say anything to you about what it's like to work at the *Standard*?"

"Yes, he did, come to think of it. He seems to be enjoying his job and apparently has a mentor."

"Did he say who?"

"No, but if I remember correctly, he said he was one of the higher-ups. He said he was a mouse who did not talk much but was keen to let him know that he valued loyalty."

CHAPTER 19

"Boxer's about to win the shot-put!" Marcus said in a loudhailer of a voice that colleagues would have once considered out of character.

Adonis, the Sports Editor, who happened to be in the newsroom, glared at him. "How do you know?" the rookie reporter asked. "How can you possibly say something like that?"

"I just know," said Marcus. "Call it a sixth sense! And I'll tell you something else… he'll do a lot better than you know who!"

The atmosphere in the *Phoenix Standard* newsroom was unusually animated that day. The Isle of Andronicus Muscle Fest was about to get under way, and Adonis was widely expected to emerge victorious in the shot, hammer throw, discus and tossing the tree trunk. Competition in the various events was open to all rodents, and arrangements had been made to accommodate competitors and others who lived outside Phoenix.

Adonis might well have demurred more forcibly after hearing Marcus's prediction had he not had more pressing matters on his mind. He had arrived at the office in his finest suit, as had the rookie reporter, and it was noticeable, too, that Phaedra was looking more elegant than ever. Iago, meanwhile, was sartorially superior to everyone, while maintaining his quietly menacing bearing. The Chairman of the Board, whose appearance remained unaltered, had been around that day and seemed to be hovering everywhere.

The Chairman rarely talked to his minions, apart from saying 'good morning' or 'good afternoon', but on this day, he stopped for a brief chat with almost everyone. After a few words with Titus – the Chief Reporter, who, as always, was tidily attired – he went round the newsroom with a conspiratorial air.

Marcus was the one to receive the most attention. "What makes you doubt that Adonis will sweep the board at the Muscle Fest?" the Chairman asked him.

"I don't know. All I know is that he won't," Marcus replied. "I can feel it in my bones."

"That's interesting," the Chairman said, in his usual, expressionless tone. "You seem to have changed since you came back from that expedition. Rumour has it that it goes back to the time when you found some ancient scrolls. Is there any truth in that, do you think?"

"I don't know, though I have a feeling that it could be the case."

"You have certainly grown in confidence! That is plain for all to see! Rumour also has it that you have acquired the powers of a clairvoyant!"

Marcus's confidence had, in fact, reached new heights. "Yes, it does seem that way," he replied. "This is something that could come in very handy on a newspaper, and I intend to make the most of it."

"That's what I like to hear," the Chairman said quietly. "Positivity!" Then he asked: "Do you know what the words on the scrolls say yet?"

"No, though I have a fair idea. I know they are important. The scrolls are with Da Vinci at present, and he's doing his best to decipher them."

"Excellent! If anyone can do it, he can. I look forward to hearing the outcome." Marcus promised to keep him informed. "Do you have any news about Cicero?" the Chairman then asked.

"Not yet, though I hope he will be out of hospital soon," Marcus told him.

The Chairman of the Board paused for a moment before changing tack. "It's a pity about poor old Caxton, isn't it?" he said.

"It certainly is," Marcus agreed. "I gather he has had a serious mental breakdown. I just hope he will recover quickly and be back with us before long." Marcus knew that he would not be back, and the Chairman knew that he knew. "It's just as well we've got Iago filling the breach, in the meantime," Marcus then said.

The Chairman responded with a 'Hmm!' before sauntering off.

The fact that Marcus had been the focus of so much attention did not go unnoticed, of course. It came as no surprise, either. The once rather timid Marcus had become the hero of the hour, and his name was often mentioned, in the office and elsewhere, in the same breath as Polo. The latter had not been seen in public lately and was said to be needing time to recuperate from the rigours of the expedition.

"I wonder if Polo's nearing the end of the road," Phaedra said to Adonis and anyone else who cared to listen. "He's getting on a bit, great explorer though he is."

Adonis nodded and said: "He's quite an icon, isn't he?"

Phaedra warmed to her theme: "The island has three icons, doesn't it? If Polo and Caxton are at or near the end of the road, that just leaves Da Vinci... and he's not exactly an adolescent!"

Phaedra's flow was interrupted by the appearance of Iago, who strode to Titus's desk, whispered a few words and then moved to where Marcus was sitting. "Well done for your efforts with the expedition" he said. "They should provide the paper with some really good stories." The tone was one of praise, albeit reluctant praise.

"How are you coping in Cicero's absence?" he then asked. After Marcus assured him everything was fine, Iago instructed him to telephone the hospital in Carthage to ascertain how Cicero was.

"I phoned the hospital yesterday and was told he would need to stay there a bit longer," Marcus replied. "I can, of course, phone again now if you wish."

After Iago departed, Marcus did exactly that. He was desperate to talk to Cicero, a kindred spirit in many ways for years, and tell him about the expedition generally and the scrolls in particular. He was convinced that the discovery carried important answers to questions Cicero had raised in the course of his research into 'The Origins of Mousekind'. Unfortunately, his call was fruitless. "No change from yesterday," he was told.

A hasty telephone call to Da Vinci followed, but the iconic inventor did not answer. With Da Vinci, it tended to be a case of 'don't call me; I'll call you', and Marcus was not in the least bit surprised.

Meanwhile, Marcus had plenty of writing to get on with. He needed to collaborate with Polo, and probably Cicero as well on some aspects, but there was no shortage of material he could get to grips with first. On top of this, there was the Muscle Fest to go to. He was particularly keen to see his expedition comrade prosper and the arrogant Adonis be pulled down a peg.

CHAPTER 20

Marcus, Rosencrantz and Boxer received heroes' welcomes as they reached their seats at The Subway Sports and Arts Centre. Four seats in the best box had been reserved for the explorers, even though two of them were not mice. Others had been set aside for Polo, Caxton, Da Vinci and the Prime Minister and his secretary. Caxton and Polo were unable to make it, Boxer was competing for much of the time and the PM and his aide made a brief appearance before leaving to attend to other duties. Da Vinci had received an invitation to attend as a matter of course, but he rarely appeared in public and was not expected to this time. As a result, Marcus and Rosencrantz had the box to themselves for most of the time.

The two conquering heroes looked downwards and around to see who else was there and to acknowledge anyone they knew. Marcus saw Phaedra and Gertrude sitting in spots that ensured they were close to the action and two reporters who were a few rows behind them. A big beam of light moved around all parts of the arena, and there were tumultuous cheers when it shone on the explorers.

The underground venue, generally known simply as 'The

Subway', had been a Da Vinci brainchild several years ago. It was centrally located and could be reached by road from all directions. A massive crater had been carved out of the earth and from this an area for sports, concerts, plays and other events of interest to the public created. Seating areas, along with kiosks where small food items could be bought, were ranged around and above this area.

As always, the event was heralded with a display of dancing to music from the town's top band by a troupe of young female hamsters. The PM then made a short speech before declaring the Muscle Fest open, and the spectators cheered loudly.

The first event, a new one, was a press-up contest. Organisers had been disappointed at the low number of participants and, in response to pleas for more, Boxer had agreed to give it a try. Adonis, on the other foot, had loftily declared that he needed to concentrate on throwing. The winner was a squat, short-limbed gerbil, who seemed able to keep going forever. After completing a thousand press-ups and realising that the other entrants had given up long ago, and that the spectators were growing restive, he decided to stop.

Weightlifting and wrestling followed. Boxer was all for competing in both but realised that, with the throwing events to follow soon afterwards, it would be prudent to at least forget about the wrestling. Competition in the weightlifting was stiff, and Boxer was pleased to finish third and receive most of the cheers. The winner, for the third year in a row, was a colossus of a lifter from Carthage.

The wrestling, always popular with the females in the audience, tended to highlight the rivalry between the rodents of Phoenix and Troy. This year was no exception, with most of the contests being between wrestlers from the two towns. The heavyweight battle was the most intensely fought of all. The spectators cheered, jeered, bayed, booed and stamped their feet as one wrestler appeared to be getting on top… and then the other. The eventual winner was the Trojan, who managed to avenge a defeat inflicted on him the previous year by the same opponent.

Next on the agenda was the shot-put, the event that most of the staff at the *Standard* had been waiting for with anticipation. For them, and many others, this was the 'Blue Riband' competition because it would feature the mighty, all-conquering Adonis. The *Standard* Sports Editor had won the shot for four years in a row, and the staff at the newspaper were in no doubt that he was about to make it five.

The one exception was Marcus. "Boxer's going to win it," he said to Rosencrantz. The gerbil, and veteran of many an adventure with Polo, had been revelling in the fact that a non-mouse was being allowed to sit in a box seat. Now he expressed surprise. He had come to increasingly respect Marcus's judgement, not to mention courage, but could not help feeling he had got it wrong this time.

Marcus could see what he was thinking. "You don't believe me, do you?" he said with a grin.

"All I can say is that you must know something I don't," Rosencrantz replied. "Adonis has dominated the throwing events for years, especially the shot. Last year, he won by a mile… and Boxer was only third!"

Marcus admitted that what Rosencrantz said was perfectly logical but then added: "I just know Boxer is going to win. Don't ask me how. I just know."

Conversations among the spectators continued to buzz for some time after the wrestling had finished, and they needed to be reminded, with the aid of a megaphone, what was taking place next. The buzz quickly quietened, and the spectators waited for their chance to cheer a hero. The name of each competitor was announced before he strode into view and acknowledged the applause that greeted him and took up a position near the shot-putting circle. Adonis, who had virtually made the event his own, was greeted with loud, reverential clapping. The loudest cheers by far, however, were reserved for Boxer.

"Stand by for a surprise!" Marcus whispered. "Boxer has grown stronger... Adonis hasn't!"

How he knew that was anyone's guess, but the prediction was spot on. Adonis turned in a below-par performance and had to settle for second place, while Boxer delivered puts that more than matched the best of previous years. The heroic hamster's victory was immensely popular, of course. It also sent shockwaves throughout The Subway, as this had been the event in which the result had been seen as a foregone conclusion. Even the organisers and stewards were dumbstruck, and there was a delay while they got their heads round what had occurred.

Everyone wanted to know what went wrong... or perhaps what went right! Almost everyone was aware that Boxer's strength had increased during the physically demanding expedition he had been on. They knew, too, that he had trained diligently before and after the expedition. However, there was no reason to believe Adonis had neglected his preparation in anything. He had been as assiduous as ever with his training regimen and made no attempt to keep that fact a secret! One or two sports pundits, who had kept their ears close to the ground, wondered whether his love life had turned sour. Adonis's trysts were less secret than he, at least, suspected! But there was no indication that anything had blunted his shot-putting ability.

"Perhaps he's just having an off day," one pundit suggested to another.

"That's something that can happen to anyone... apart from Adonis!" the other replied.

Among the most delighted of the spectators was Rosencrantz, who sat silently in a state of open-mouthed euphoria. Marcus could not conceal his amusement. "What did I tell you?!" he said with a smirk.

Next on the programme was a short display by a group of gymnasts, who demonstrated their strength with exercises on parallel bars, pull-ups, pyramids and rope-climbing feats. The spectators were respectfully asked to stop talking while the display was taking place.

After that came the discus-throwing competition, in which Adonis was again the firm favourite. Boxer was beginning to tire as a result of earlier endeavours, but he was still able to beat the favourite into third place. The winner was a gerbil from Troy, who had been the runner-up to Adonis at the two previous meetings. There were more gasps from the spectators as the competitors performed and Adonis looked out of sorts. The one spectator who was not surprised in the least was, inevitably, Marcus, while Rosencrantz was prepared to believe anything!

A music and movement display by twenty middle-aged females then took place, while the hammer throwers prepared themselves for the penultimate event. Word went round that

Adonis, again the favourite, had left The Subway in a state of high dudgeon. Boxer decided to take a rest, and the winner, tipped in advance by Marcus, was a Trojan mouse.

Marcus was also uncannily correct in predicting who would win the tree-tossing contest. This was the curtain closer and a new event. How Marcus could know the outcome was beyond belief, as the rodent who emerged victorious was a handsome young hamster who lived on a farm near Carthage, and no one, it seemed, had ever heard of him. A refreshed Boxer took part in this, too, and finished a creditable second… as Marcus knew he would! No winner and runner-up had endeared themselves so much to the public before, and the spectators were able to go home in a happy frame of mind.

CHAPTER 21

Circulation soared as soon as Marcus's reports about his adventure started to appear in the *Phoenix Standard*. The reports were vivid, descriptive, even lyrical, and they sent pulses racing. Colleagues felt compelled to express admiration for Marcus's work, and both Phaedra and Gertrude began to flutter their eyelids in his presence. Phaedra, the Features Editor, who was still officially in overall charge of the expedition reportage, let Marcus get on with it for the most part. She had other fish to fry.

The Chairman of the Board had circulated a notice to the effect that Caxton would be absent for a long time and that a review of the editorial staffing would take place soon. Most of the mice in the newsroom concluded that Caxton would not be coming back at all, and inevitably, many cast their eyes on a potential promotion ladder.

"I suppose Iago will be the one to take over as Editor," the rookie reporter said.

"Not necessarily," one of his older colleagues observed. "It could be someone from outside." Phaedra pointed out that if Iago was to move up, he would need a deputy.

"Someone like you, I suppose!" said Marcus, who then asked Titus for his views on the subject.

"All I know is that I'm happy where I am," the Chief Reporter replied.

The statement by Titus meant that, as far as anyone knew, there were three internal names in the frame: Iago, Phaedra and Adonis. There had been speculation that the latter two would be vying for promotion on a 'joint ticket'. However, relations between the pair had soured visibly recently, and a three-horse race was envisaged… or, with Adonis seemingly out of favour in some quarters, just a two-horse one.

It soon became apparent that Adonis was not popular with Iago, when the Deputy Editor and Acting Editor strode into the newsroom and berated the Sports Editor for how he had covered the Muscle Fest. "What you have written is sloppy, sub-standard and amateurish," Iago said with lacerating contempt. "It's as pathetic as the way you performed at the Fest. What's the matter with you?! Have you been so busy sulking about how you did that you felt there was no need to write it up properly?" For one uneasy moment, it looked as if Adonis was going to hit Iago. Instead, he burst into tears and fled.

After Adonis had gone, Iago glared at those who remained where they were. To say he had got out of the wrong side of his bed was putting it mildly! "What are you all staring at?!" he snarled. "There's a lot of work to be done… so get on with it!" He then took up residence at the desk normally occupied by Cicero and continued to glare at everyone.

On noticing that Marcus appeared to be unmoved by what had occurred, he asked him whether he had managed to contact Polo yet. Marcus looked hard into Iago's eyes before replying. "Not yet, though you can rest assured that I will keep on trying."

"Any news about Cicero?" Iago then asked.

"No," said Marcus. "I wish there was. I'm particularly keen to talk to him."

Iago began to bristle. "Make sure you keep on it," he ordered. "It's especially important that you get hold of Polo. Phaedra needs to talk to him, too."

A moment later, Gertrude's telephone rang, and the news desk secretary told Marcus that Da Vinci wanted to see him. "Great! I want to see him, too," Marcus declared, as he got up and left the room. Iago's baleful eyes followed him as he went before they rested on all the others present in turn.

* * *

Da Vinci was waiting just inside his workshop door when Marcus arrived. He had rarely, if ever, asked anyone to see him and could not conceal his delight. "Come with me," he said with a grin so wide that it almost obliterated his face.

He led Marcus to the Flying Machine, which was now undraped and at ground level. It was gleaming and glistening under the influence of polish and elbow grease. "There you are!" the great inventor said. "It's as clean as a new pin and, more importantly, ready to go."

"Does this mean you're all set for take-off?" Marcus asked, without needing to.

"Absolutely!" Da Vinci roared, with an undisguised sense of triumph. "You are looking at something that is going to revolutionise the way we are all going to live… and I would be flying yesterday, if that was possible!"

"What about tomorrow?" Marcus asked, tongue in cheek.

"What about now?!" Da Vinci's grin grew even wider, and the workshop looked set to shake under the power of his decibels. "What about now?!" he said again. Marcus felt the adrenaline surge through his veins, as he knew what was about to happen next.

"There's nothing to stop us," Da Vinci added in a more thoughtful tone. "Unusually for this time of year, the climactic conditions outside are not too bad at all, and it should be perfectly safe to fly. I feel the climate is changing, anyway. I know a way out of here that no one else knows about, and I want to take my new creation on a test flight."

"That's a great story for the *Standard*," Marcus said. "Are you happy for me to write something about it?"

Da Vinci burst out laughing. "Of course! What's more, I want you to come with me… to take to the air with me!" he exclaimed. "Why do you think you're here?!"

Now it was Marcus's turn to grin broadly. "When do we start?" he asked eagerly. "And how do we get the Flying Machine out into the open?"

Da Vinci was jumping up and down in a way that contradicted his image of a wise, albeit eccentric, mouse of advancing years. "How does going right this minute grab you?" he asked, with the biggest grin yet.

Without ado, he moved to one side of his workshop and pressed a button on an otherwise bare wall. There was a shaking sound and a space appeared at the bottom. The wall gradually disappeared to reveal a massive hole, beyond which was a wide and gentle metallic slope.

Da Vinci got into the Flying Machine, via a tiny ladder, and motioned Marcus to follow. Inside were four seats, two at the front and two behind, and a small space for storing luggage and equipment at the back. Da Vinci pressed a button in the centre of a dashboard to make the machine move up the slope. The engine made a noise like a trio of tractors, while underneath the machine the screeching of tyres rubbing against metal could be heard. There was the smell of burning rubber, too. As the machine approached the top of the slope, Da Vinci pressed another button and a giant corrugated iron door slid open to reveal an expanse of sky.

Outside was a large, concrete square. Da Vinci steered the machine onto the square, turned the engine off and got out to close the corrugated door. Marcus looked out onto a part of Phoenix he was unfamiliar with. He could see no signs of outdoor activity, which was to be expected during the Cold Season. However, there were none of the usual blizzards and it was not particularly cold.

"Our moment has arrived!" Da Vinci declared, after clambering back inside. "We are about to get a bird's-eye view of our town." He pressed a big, red button directly in front of him, and the whirring of blades above could be heard. "I want you to watch what I am doing," Da Vinci added. "Someone else apart from me needs to learn how to use the machine… and it might as well be you!"

A couple of minutes later, they were airborne. At first, the machine rose vertically until all the buildings below resembled toys. Da Vinci then turned his attention to a large wheel that could be reached easily by both pilot and passenger.

"Now, watch what I'm doing," Da Vinci said, as he turned the wheel to the left and made the machine head in that direction. Marcus, who made sure he took this in, observed that the sky was grey with a few clouds just visible, but in no way turbulent as would normally have been expected during this season. He then looked downwards and kept an eye open for landmarks. The Big Cheese Stadium and the roads leading to it soon came into view. Although they appeared tiny from where he was, Marcus could see what a prominent feature they were in Phoenix. He saw the Town Hall, too, along with some of the houses that stood on stilts, and he even got a sighting of the main above-ground premises of the *Standard*.

"Let's have a quick look at the coastline," Da Vinci said suddenly. The machine veered off in a different direction and Phoenix was soon just a blob on the horizon behind. The coast came into view surprisingly quickly, and Marcus was enthralled to see how imposing were the cliffs that surrounded the island. And the size of the sea was awesome. The water stretched ahead, as well as to either side, endlessly and without interruption. Long beads of foam and rearing waves appeared formidable even from a distance.

"Right! Time for you to have a drive!" Da Vinci barked, without warning. "As you can see, it's quite easy." He used a lever to adjust the positions of the dashboard and wheel and then added: "I suggest you take us home!"

Marcus, who had been carefully watching what Da Vinci did as well as observing the island's topography, proved to be a highly capable pupil. He took to flying like a duck to water, though he did now need to focus on the flight and nothing else.

As the Flying Machine approached the point where it had taken off, Da Vinci took over again. "I'm sure you can do this bit, but it's best to play it safe," he said. The machine descended slowly at ninety degrees onto the spot from which it had taken off. Da Vinci got out to open the giant door that it had to go through again and guided the machine gently down the metal slope and back into his workshop.

"How are you feeling?" Da Vinci asked as they sat at a table close to where the machine stood once more.

"Exhilarated!" Marcus replied.

"That's excellent!" the inventor said. "This is just the beginning! I have big plans for the Flying Machine, all sorts of plans. Some of them will undoubtedly involve our friend, Polo."

"Have you heard from him lately?" Marcus asked. "I have been trying to get in touch with him urgently but without success."

"Me too," said Da Vinci. "That's one little problem we need to overcome." Da Vinci grinned again, though Marcus suddenly detected a tired look and realised that he should not overstay his welcome.

Before leaving, however, there was still a matter to be resolved. "You might recall that the last time I was here, I left some ancient scrolls with you," he said. "Have you had a chance to look at them?"

"Oh, my goodness!" Da Vinci exclaimed. "Yes, I have, and amid all the excitement that's been going on, I forgot all about them." He went to a cupboard, fished out the scrolls and photographed papers, and put them on the table.

"I don't know if this is of any use to you, but I have been able to decipher a bit of the lettering on one of the scrolls with the help of some special dust that I had invented to help magnify things," he said, as he unrolled the scroll in question. "I have no idea of what the picture is of, except that it is not of a rodent, but I can show you a bit of lettering… though what it means is beyond me!"

Marcus could see that beside the drawing, which was on the right, were two lines of capital letters. On the top line were four letters, the first two of which were H and O. The bottom line consisted of six, or possibly seven, letters. The first two were S and A and the fifth looked like an I.

"I don't know if that helps at all, but that's it, I'm afraid," said Da Vinci.

"I don't know for sure either, but I have a feeling this could be really useful," Marcus replied. "What I really need to do now is show this wording to Cicero… if only I could."

Marcus thanked Da Vinci for his help, not to mention his remarkable hospitality, and made to leave. Before he did, the latter had something else to say: "You know where we're flying next, don't you?"

"I don't," said Marcus, "but I would love to be part of your plans."

"We're going to The Oven," Da Vinci told him. "That's right, The Oven, the place where no one had dared to enter… until now! The plan includes you, me, Polo and perhaps one other. I aim to set it all up as soon as I can get hold of Polo."

Marcus's mood became more upbeat than ever, though he could not fail to notice that his host was looking worryingly weary.

CHAPTER 22

"Where have you been?!" Iago asked angrily.

"Up in the air!" Marcus replied nonchalantly.

"Are you trying to be funny?" the Deputy Editor asked. "What do you mean by that? I will ask you again: where have you *been*?!"

Marcus had never seen the cool, but quietly menacing, Iago act like this before. He could sense that his lack of customary control stemmed from insecurity. He was not entirely sure what had caused this, though it was not hard to hazard a guess.

Marcus, who was in full control himself and feeling anything but insecure, knew that he had the upper hand for a change.

"I have been flying with Da Vinci," he said. Iago, who was now more nonplussed than ever, asked him to 'kindly explain'.

"I had a phone call from Da Vinci, saying he wanted to see me," Marcus told him. "As you know, he's normally very elusive. As you also know – at least I assume you know – he has been working on creating a Flying Machine. Well, the machine is now ready, and Da Vinci and I have been up in it on a test flight." Iago stood open-mouthed and, for a moment, was at a loss for words.

"I think you will agree that this is a major story," Marcus added. "This is something that will affect just about everyone on the island… and there's more to come. Da Vinci wants me to join him on a flight to The Oven. He wants Polo to be on the flight, too. Da Vinci and Polo have talked, in the past, about a possible air trip to The Oven. I know Polo is desperate to give it another go. He regards it as unfinished business. Now, it's a real possibility."

At this point, Gertrude called out across the newsroom: "We've managed to make contact with Polo. He's keen to talk to you."

"We have had quite a job getting hold of him, but he's now ready to be interviewed," Titus added. "Phaedra can handle Polo's take on things, as you have plenty else on your plate. You obviously need to write a piece about the test flight, the Flying Machine itself and how it is likely to affect all our lives. And there's that planned trip to The Oven as well!" Titus asked Iago if he approved of what he had just said.

Iago gave a cursory nod, before rounding on Marcus again. "I still expect staff to keep me informed of their whereabouts," he told him.

"Don't be so stupid!" Marcus retorted curtly. "I have been unearthing major stories for the newspaper, and I don't have to tell the whole of Andronicus and his wife!"

Almost everyone in the newsroom stared at the pair in disbelief. No one had ever dared to speak to Iago in this manner before, and no one was more stunned than Iago. The Deputy Editor froze on the spot for a moment before storming back to his office.

In so doing, he almost collided with the Chairman of the Board, who had been standing quietly in a corner. "What was that all about?" the Chairman asked no one in particular, after Iago had disappeared. "As if I didn't know!"

The Chairman and Phaedra took care not to collide with each other as he departed and she arrived. The Features Editor was all smiles. "How's the hero of the hour?" she asked Marcus, with a flutter of the eyelids.

"He has become an even bigger hero since you last saw him," said Gertrude, who went on to describe the run-in he had just had with Iago.

"My goodness!" Phaedra exclaimed. "The once-timid Marcus has become a true superhero! That Iago is a nasty piece of work, and it's high time he was pulled down a peg!"

Titus, who clearly did not want to get involved in this or any other personality clash, cleared his throat and reminded everyone that there was an exceptional amount of work to be done.

But Phaedra refused to be denied. "I have something important to tell you about Caxton and Iago," she declared.

Titus cut in by asking Phaedra if she had managed to contact Polo. "I have arranged to interview Polo… who I have a feeling is not very well at the moment… and will be dealing with that shortly," she replied. "I have also phoned Cicero, by the way."

"How is Cicero?" Marcus asked. "I have been trying to contact him myself, as you know."

"Oh, he was wittering on about the 'Origins of Mousekind', as usual and saying that there are big changes afoot that will affect the whole island," she said. "He sounded dippier and more doddery than ever!"

"Did he give you any idea of when he would be coming back?" Titus asked.

"When's Caxton coming back, for that matter?" said Gertrude.

"That brings me to the most important thing I have to tell you," Phaedra replied, with a conspiratorial air that easily overrode Titus's air of resignation regarding getting work done.

"As you know, there have been rumours that Iago has been trying to usurp Caxton by stabbing him in the back," she went on. "Well, it very much looks as if those rumours are true."

"How can you possibly know that?" asked Titus, who could not conceal his interest any longer.

"Did you know Caxton had been having marital problems?" Phaedra asked everyone. "Yes? Well, guess who's been having a paw in them!"

"What, you mean Iago?!" one of the reporters asked.

"Got it in one!" said Phaedra, who was warming to her theme.

"What did he do, exactly?" another reporter asked.

Phaedra paused for a moment to ensure she had everyone's attention.

"Iago had been stalking Caxton's wife, Ophelia," she said. "He has been following her, or getting someone else to follow her on his behalf, wherever she went... presumably to see if he could dig up some dirt on her." Everyone in the room was now fascinated to know what Phaedra was going to say next, and no one noticed that the rookie reporter was hiding his face behind a copy of the *Standard*.

"At first, the stalking came to nothing, and Iago was about to give up... until one day, when Ophelia was seen heading in the direction of The Slum," Phaedra continued. "I don't know how many of you have met Ophelia, but if you had, you would not believe that someone with such an aristocratic bearing would go to such a place. However, go to The Slum she did… and Iago followed her."

"Why would she go there?!" an astonished Gertrude asked.

"She was seen meeting and embracing a young male mouse. Caxton knew nothing about this until Iago somehow tipped him the wink. He would have done it subtly, that's for sure! Ophelia was subsequently seen with the same young male many times, and Caxton was led to believe the pair were secret lovers."

"If they were not lovers, what were they?" Marcus asked.

Phaedra paused again before delivering the denouement. "The young male was not her lover… but her *son*!" she declared, with a dramatic wave. "He was the product of a secret affair she had had with a rodent far below her station and long before meeting Caxton. And she didn't want Caxton to know about it."

"How do you know all this?" Titus asked.

"As it happens, one or two of my contacts live or work in The Slum. Ophelia's son is known to them. One of my contacts has met Ophelia, and another has seen Iago or someone younger loitering in the vicinity."

"How much does Caxton know of all this?" Marcus asked. "And how much, I wonder, has it affected him?"

"I understand that the whole business has driven a wedge between Caxton and Ophelia. Their marriage is reported to be in tatters. Ophelia has walked out on him, and Caxton is said to be devastated."

"Are they still apart?"

"I don't know for sure, though I have heard that there has been a complete breakdown between them."

"Something tells me that Caxton's mental state is not good and that Iago is poised to take over officially as Editor," said Marcus. "I hope I'm wrong, of course."

"That's food for thought, to say the least," said Phaedra. "I suppose we will all have to wait and see. Anyway, I thought you would like to hear about the latest scandal!"

"We're always in the market for a scandal!" one of the reporters quipped.

The Features Editor picked up her pawbag and notebook and, on leaving, added: "Meanwhile, I have an explorer to see!"

A stunned silence followed, after which a harassed-looking Titus pleaded with the others to get some work done.

Marcus had more to do than most, but before going back to writing up his description of the Flying Machine and the test flight he had been on, he decided to make another attempt at contacting Cicero on the telephone. This time, he was successful. "It's wonderful to hear from you," his colleague said. "I have been convalescing in Carthage but hope to be back soon."

"That's brilliant!" Marcus said. "It's good to hear you're getting better, and we must get together soon. There are all sorts of things we have to talk about."

Marcus was about to expand on what those things were, when Titus tapped him on the shoulder.

"The Chairman of the Board wants to see you in his office," the Chief Reporter told him.

No one was meant to know, but one of the reporters somehow did, and so, too, did the rest of the room in an instant… and everyone was stunned for a second time. Requests or summonses to be seen in the Chairman's office had hitherto been unheard of.

Marcus told Cicero he had to go. "Sorry about this, but believe it or not, 'God' wants to see me in his office!" he said, sounding genuinely surprised. Everyone watched and no one said a word as Marcus left the room.

Getting to the Chairman's office entailed walking up a small flight of steps to one side of the newsroom and knocking on an iron door at the top that remained locked for almost all of the time. The door was opened from the inside by a burly hamster in a navy-blue uniform, who led Marcus along a small, carpeted corridor to a polished oak door at the end. The security officer knocked on the door and said: "Your appointment is here, Sir." A middle-aged female mouse opened the door and invited Marcus to enter.

"Thank you for coming. Please take a seat," the Chairman said from behind a monolith of a desk. He waved towards a large, leather chair on the other side of the desk and directly opposite to him. Marcus noticed that, apart from the desk, there was nothing unusual about the office. It was neat, not especially large and, as might be expected, contained a table laden with new and old copies of the *Phoenix Standard*. There were half a dozen other chairs, photographs of Phoenix on a board that hung on one of the pink-painted walls and a wall-to-wall blue carpet chosen for durability rather than beauty. On the desk were a couple of trophies, a family photograph and three wire trays filled with paperwork.

"I understand that you have become quite a celebrity," the Chairman said in his customary monotone. As always, his square, white face showed not even a flicker of emotion.

He was a middle-class, middle-aged mouse of average height, average build and even average dress sense. He could, and did, go around anywhere unnoticed, and it was almost impossible to guess what was on his mind.

"Thank you," said Marcus. "Going on that expedition was an experience I will never forget."

"The public won't forget, either," the Chairman said. "It is our job to make sure that they don't. Do you not agree?"

"Absolutely!"

"Good! I also hear you have been up in the newly invented Flying Machine and that you now have plans to enter The Oven. Is that right?"

"Yes, and I must admit that I'm looking forward to that immensely."

"That's excellent," the Chairman said, as deadpan as ever. "When you have done that, you will be as famous as Polo… perhaps even more so. And that has to be good for the paper."

Marcus, who was now pretty sure why he had been summoned, replied, tongue in cheek: "That doesn't make me feel so bad, either!"

The Chairman remained impassive. "The trouble is that some other recent events have been anything but good. I am talking about Caxton in particular. He has been a wonderful figurehead for the *Standard* for a long time, with the kind of charisma that none of the other higher-ups come even close to matching. Unfortunately, as you know, he has been cracking up lately. I have been told he has had a complete mental breakdown, and it looks as if he might have to leave. I am keeping his job open for the moment but might need to find a replacement in the near future."

"I should imagine Iago will be the one to take over, won't

he?" Marcus asked, without believing it for a moment. He thought what he said might elicit a visible reaction, but he was wrong.

"Iago is the natural successor, of course. At least he is on paper. But I'm not so sure. I have heard that Iago put it about that Caxton's wife had been unfaithful to him. My source tells me that Iago has, for some time, been trying to undermine him and that the alleged infidelity played a part in causing Caxton's breakdown. That is not good. This is something that could become public knowledge, and I am not at all sure that I want someone like Iago becoming the face of the *Phoenix Standard*."

"If Iago's not going to do it, who will?" asked Marcus, who was trying to match the Chairman's deadpan.

"There are not many options internally, I'm afraid," the Chairman replied. "There is Adonis, who has personality but is immature and is not suitable for that reason. There's Titus, who is very good at what he does but lacks personality. I have a feeling he wouldn't want the job, anyway. So that leaves Phaedra. She's duplicitous, of course, but that's not necessarily such a bad thing."

"You indicated that the appointment might go to a candidate from another paper. Is that likely?"

"That's a possibility, though I would prefer the appointment to be internal."

A long pause followed, during which Marcus knew what the Chairman was going to say next… and the Chairman knew that he knew.

"There is one other possibility," the Chairman said at length. "The rodents who read the *Standard* like to have a figurehead… someone with charisma… at the helm, someone they feel they can relate to, as well as look up to. As I said earlier, you are about to become as famous as Polo, a household name. You might be just the sort of personality that is needed here. You have changed so much since the expedition. You just might be the right mouse for the job."

"That's incredibly flattering!" Marcus said, in an attempt to sound surprised.

The Chairman stood up, walked to the door and held it open for Marcus to walk through. "I think you will agree that we both have a lot to think about," he said in a tone that still refused to deviate. "In the meantime, good luck with The Oven."

CHAPTER 23

There were surprises in store for Marcus when he arrived at Da Vinci's workshop in readiness for the flight to The Oven. He had had another practice flight since his first visit to the workshop. So, too, had Polo, by all accounts. Now it was time for the 'big one'.

Polo had arrived already and so, too, to Marcus's surprise, had Cicero, as well as Rosencrantz and Boxer. "I'm here to wish you luck," said Cicero. "I thought it was the least I could do, since we keep missing each other."

Marcus, who quickly guessed why the other two were present, expressed delight at seeing all three.

"We have quite a bit to talk about," he then said to Cicero.

"We certainly do!" the veteran Feature Writer exclaimed. "What I can tell you now is that I'm almost certain that the scrolls and other stuff you found are related to some sort of super mammal of the past, a mammal that reigned supreme long before the rodents took over. I suspect that these mammals reigned for longer than we mice have. And it would not surprise me if there were other islands that they ruled, as well as Andronicus."

"How did you arrive at such a conclusion?" asked Polo, who was starting to fidget. Apart from being sceptical, he was keen to get his latest outing under way... especially this one.

Cicero winced and scratched the top of his hairless head. "I don't know," he said. "I just have a very strong feeling that I'm right. The climate is changing, there are changes afoot at the *Standard* and I'm convinced that mice will not be rulers forever. Nothing is constant!"

At this point, Marcus sensed that the others were growing restive and wanted to be airborne as soon as possible. "We must have a really good natter when we get back," he said to Cicero.

Da Vinci took this suggestion as a cue to address the others. "I have reluctantly reached the conclusion that I am too old to go on such a hazardous and physically demanding expedition," he announced. Marcus could see that he bore a distinct air of weariness.

"This is why Boxer and I are both here," Rosencrantz said.

"That's right," said Da Vinci. "I quite simply don't feel up to it, which is why I have brought in the two of you as back-up for Polo and Marcus."

"Presumably Cicero is here as a ground-level guest!" Marcus quipped.

"Quite so," said Da Vinci.

"Are we all set to go?" Polo then asked, still agitated. Marcus sensed that the legendary explorer was still far from fully fit, and this worried him.

Da Vinci echoed these thoughts by asking Polo if he was sure he was all right.

"Leading an expedition to The Oven has been a life-long ambition, and I'm not missing it for anything!" The great adventurer was visibly incensed.

"That's great!" said Boxer. "We've got the same old team together again!"

"All right, let's not waste any more time!" Da Vinci then said, with a wave towards his latest, and arguably greatest, invention. As the quartet of explorers boarded the Flying Machine, Da Vinci invited Cicero to stay for a while. "I would very much like to hear you expand on what you said a minute ago about nothing being constant," he told him.

Da Vinci and Cicero watched as Polo, sitting at the front with Marcus, revved up the engine and steered the machine out of the workshop in the way both he and Marcus had been taught.

"There goes my prototype," Da Vinci said with a sigh once his latest creation had disappeared. "I only hope it comes back in one piece."

Cicero nodded and added: "I hope and pray that all its occupants come back safely as well."

Da Vinci voiced agreement with an "Absolutely!"

As the Flying Machine left its subterranean berth and then rose vertically into the sky, a loud cheer came from a throng of onlookers who had opted to brave the elements and wish the explorers well. The explorers did not hear, though they could see the crowd below and that many of the onlookers were waving. The weather conditions, meanwhile, remained unusually mild, and visibility was good.

As the machine headed towards its destination, the quartet were able to look at Phoenix's landmarks again and, later, those of Troy. The topography of the slightly smaller Troy was, in many ways, similar to that of Phoenix. Troy had its own, albeit smaller, version of the Big Cheese Stadium, a town hall of much the same style and a similar road layout.

Under the circumstances, it was perhaps surprising that so much animosity existed between the two towns. The citizens of Phoenix regarded the Trojans as socially and culturally inferior, while the Trojans believed their Phoenix counterparts to be snobbish and slightly decadent. In reality, there was more wealth and a higher proportion of upper-class mice in Phoenix. Troy, on the other foot, had a higher proportion of gerbils and hamsters. Many Trojans resented being part of a smaller community, and they sought to compensate by trying to better their rivals at sporting events.

Before long, Troy became a speck on the landscape as the Flying Machine approached The Oven. The quartet could look down onto the rooftops of villages and farms and, of course, masses of open space. There was even a fleeting sighting of Polo's home.

The last major landmark was Carthage, the sight of which evoked fond memories. "How about dropping in for a chat with the mayor and a bite to eat?" Rosencrantz suggested with a grin. Marcus and Boxer were amused, but Polo remained po-faced.

"The plan is to touch down in or near The Oven and not before," Polo pointed out sternly. "And we still have some way to go."

'Some way to go' was, in fact, something of an understatement. Polo and Marcus took it in turns to steer the Flying Machine over mile upon mile of uncharted territory. The territory was, for the most part, wasteland... which eventually became desert. The air temperature climbed steadily, though the heat was less intense and oppressive than had been expected. The journey continued in silence for several hours until the two pilots began to tire, and twilight became imminent. So, the Flying Machine was brought down onto the expanse of parched earth that lay below.

There was no sand at this point, just dry, grey earth. There was no sign of any kind of life either, save a couple of cacti and a solitary blade of grass acting in defiance against the elements. The four explorers availed themselves of some of the provisions they had brought and then slept where they sat.

The light and sight of the rising sun at dawn was all that was needed to wake them. The quartet, still sitting where they were, had a slightly hurried breakfast, after which Marcus said to Polo: "I should imagine we are just a few hours away from The Oven."

Polo gave a cursory nod. "Would you mind doing the driving for now?" he then asked.

Before taking to the sky once more, Marcus asked the other two whether they were still 'fit and firing', and they both confirmed that they were as eager as ever. Polo, meanwhile, went back to sleep and remained asleep for the rest of the flight.

The second part of the expedition took about six hours, with the terrain below remaining unremittingly arid throughout. Eventually, something could be seen on the horizon that was higher than ground level. As the quartet gradually drew close, they could see a long row of towering rocks. As they approached touching distance, it became apparent that the rocks, which were almost tall enough to be cliffs, were forming a massive square. The rocks themselves resembled giant sentinels charged with the task of guarding what lay inside. A ring of red-hot embers could be seen in front of the rocks and were arguably acting as an extra line of defence.

Marcus gave Polo a gentle nudge. "I think we are here," he said quietly.

Polo yawned and nodded. "That's right," he confirmed. "We are now outside The Oven."

Marcus brought the Flying Machine down to a spot that was well back from the embers. "We don't want to come back from The Oven to find our transport has been burned to a crisp," he observed. "Da Vinci wouldn't be very pleased, either!"

CHAPTER 24

It was now a matter of finding a way through the rocks. The quartet were relieved that the temperature was lower than expected, but the heat was still quite oppressive, and the presence of embers made it essential for them to watch their feet at all times as they walked round. Eventually, they found a gap that turned out to be a tunnel. The tunnel was in fact about half a mile long. It was narrow, with a sometimes low ceiling, and Boxer, in particular, found progress hard going.

At the end was a rocky, rubble-strewn slope than ran down at about forty-five degrees for a hundred feet. At the bottom was a flat area that seemed to stretch forever in every direction.

Boxer announced that he needed a rest before descending. With his burly frame, he had suffered more than the others from the tunnel's claustrophobic pressure cooker of an atmosphere. Polo, who had been the first to enter and who had led the quartet along it, was in a bad way as well. "I have to stop for a moment," he said, while gasping and wheezing.

Rosencrantz could not conceal his concern. "I have never seen our leader like this before," he said to Marcus quietly, when he had a chance. "I have a feeling that, sooner or later, you are going to need to take over."

The quartet used their enforced break to consume some of the food and water they had brought along, before making their way down the slope. The heat intensified with every downwards step. The sun was beating downwards, and the monolithic rocks around The Oven were trapping the heat inside. The sun's rays were particularly savage at the bottom, and the four explorers immediately cast their eyes around in search of some sort of respite.

Rosencrantz saw what he thought was a gap in the rocks to the right. The quartet trudged towards it and, after a short climb, discovered a passage that looked similar to the one they had been through a little earlier. By the time they reached it, they were sweating copiously and in need of another rest. Polo, in particular, was gasping for breath.

A pleasant surprise awaited them, however. The passage they had just reached was shorter, wider and, more importantly, remarkably cool. To the amazement of all, a stream of almost icy air was there to greet them. "Who would have guessed that The Oven had a ventilation system!" Marcus quipped. In echoing the thoughts of everyone, he wondered whether this was a case of many a true word being said in jest.

The cool air proved to be the perfect tonic, and the quartet proceeded with renewed vigour. The passage took them to a small, cell-like room on a corner and a wider passage to the left. Along this passage, more rooms could be found at fifty-foot intervals. The rooms were all of a similar size and style to the first one they had seen, and most had doors to them.

"This reminds me a bit of the Rats' Palace," Marcus observed.

"Me too," said Polo. "I wonder if we're going to meet some more rats. It's a very different habitat this time, of course."

The quartet continued along the passage, which seemed to be endless, or at least long enough to occupy one entire side of The Oven. After a while, however, steps could be seen, and these led to an area that resembled the landing of a house and more rooms. The rooms were larger than those seen earlier, but like the others, were empty. The area as a whole looked spic and span but contained absolutely nothing. So, it was a matter of back down the steps and back along the passage, with more empty rooms to the side and no sign of life.

On the plus side were the facts that the air remained fresh and that the passage remained high and wide enough for progress to continue comfortably, albeit with the aid of torches. However, walking along a cool passage with not a great deal to see was not what the four explorers had travelled to The Oven for. Polo echoed these thoughts as loudly as he could by saying: "All I have discovered so far has been a sense of frustration."

His voice boomed along the route ahead, and then, without warning, all four explorers were made to almost jump out of their skins when they heard an even louder voice.

"What is it that you want?!" the voice said. It was shrill and sounded angry.

They had no idea where it had come from until, a few minutes later, they came to a second flight of steps.

"Go away! You are not welcome here!" the voice said from above. An outline that most rodents had only seen in school textbooks came into view.

"Good grief!" Marcus exclaimed. "It's a shrew!"

"Yes, that's right, I am a shrew! I don't suppose any of you have ever seen one before! Now, go away!"

The four explorers looked at each other for a moment before deciding to ignore what they regarded as a petulant directive and made their way up the steps. The shrew took a few paces backwards, and the quartet could see that the shrew was female, probably of late middle age and just over five feet tall. Around half a dozen younger, taller shrews of each gender then emerged from various doors and stood with her as the interlopers approached.

"I am sorry if we have upset you," said Polo, who had remained subdued for a long time but decided now was the time to take the initiative. "We did not mean to, and we have come as friends. My name is Polo, and my companions are Marcus, Rosencrantz and Boxer. We have come from Phoenix to explore The Oven and all we want to do is learn what we can... and be your friends."

"My name is Catherine, though everyone here knows me as the Matriarch," the shrew replied in a tone that was far from friendly. "I am the one who makes sure that the other shrews here stay safe. Since when has a mouse wanted to be friends with a shrew?"

"Why do you say something like that?" Boxer asked innocently. "Why are you treating us like enemies?"

The Matriarch, whose eyes were growing redder by the second, responded with withering contempt. "You are not very bright, are you?" she said. "Even for a hamster! It's easy to see that all your brains are in your biceps!"

"There's no need for that!" protested Marcus. "We are just explorers looking to learn about a part of the island we haven't seen before."

The Matriarch ignored the protest and fixed her focus on Polo. "I can see from the way you have been fidgeting that you know why we are less than delighted to see you. You are certainly old enough, and you might even be bright enough!"

"I'm old enough, if nothing else," Polo admitted. "I have memories of one or two shrews being around when I was very young. But then, no more…"

"And you know why that is, don't you?"

"Yes, I believe I do," Polo replied with an air of humility that was far from contrived.

"You *believe* you do?!" The Matriarch glared at Polo and then at each of the other three before turning to the other shrews and saying: "Well, how about that! We have got a mouse who *believes* he knows why we are less than pleased to see him!" The other shrews cheered and jeered.

Once the noise had died down, Marcus made a plea for tolerance. "The four of us are not responsible for what happened in the past. I wish we could find some way we could turn back the clock and change things, but we can't."

The Matriarch went into a huddle with the other shrews, before asking the quartet: "What is it exactly you are looking for, and what is it you want from us?" The tone was less hostile now but still extremely suspicious.

"All we seek is friendship," said Marcus.

"What, nothing else? Nothing at all?" The Matriarch sounded sceptical, to say the least. "Come on, there must be something you're after! How about gold, for example?"

"That's something that does interest us," Polo admitted. "I don't really know why, but some mice seem to put value on it… but have no idea of what to do with it. There are some who say gold has some historical importance attached to it, but no one has any idea what that is."

"We have a chest full of gold," one of the Matriarch's

minions said. "It has gold coins, gold bars, golden goblets and gold watches. And you're not having any of them!"

"We don't want them," said Boxer.

"I am interested to know what, if anything, you intend to do with it all," Rosencrantz added.

"We keep the chest of gold because it serves as a reminder of what has happened in the past," the Matriarch said. "It ensures that we never forget the awfulness of it all."

"What's that got to do with us?" Marcus asked, a little impatiently.

"No one said it did!" The Matriarch's eyes reddened again. "You mice really think you're something, don't you?!"

"All right," said Polo. "If the gold has got nothing to do with us, whose concern is it exactly?" The attitude of the shrews was beginning to irritate him.

"Has it ever occurred to you that the Isle of Andronicus might have once been ruled by beings other than mice... long before mice came along and took over?" the Matriarch asked, as if issuing a challenge.

"It has to me," said Marcus. "I have a friend who has been studying our origins for almost all his life, and he has often talked about that possibility."

"Now there's a mouse I would like to meet! I never ever thought I would say that! Your friend is right. I believe that very strongly. I also believe that whatever sort of being it was had far more power than any kind of rodent... and reigned supreme for far, far longer."

"What made this being lose its power, do you think?" asked Marcus. "Why does that being not exist now?"

"That's a fair point," the Matriarch conceded. "My own theory is that these beings were wiped out by some sort of holocaust… a holocaust that they could see coming but chose to ignore."

"That idea is really fascinating. My friend's name is Cicero, and it would be wonderful if you could get together with him somehow."

"If you think I'm going all the way to Phoenix to talk to an infernal mouse, you must be bonkers! If he wants to talk to me, he can come over here!"

"That won't be possible, I'm afraid. He is not well at present, and he's also getting on a bit. So, he wouldn't be up to the journey."

"Pity! Cicero sounds interesting. He might be the one mouse I could have a bit of time for!"

"Are you sure we can't persuade you to come back with us?" Marcus knew the answer already but felt it was worth one more try. In any case, if the Matriarch took a place in the Flying Machine, he or one of his companions would have to stay behind.

The Matriarch snorted. "I might have time for Cicero but whether I do for you is another matter!"

"We are sorry to hear that," said Polo. "We have no wish to cause you offence, and if that's really the way you feel, perhaps we should be on our way."

The Matriarch's first reaction was to say, "Good!" But then, after a pause, she asked: "Where will you go?"

"Our plan is simply to see what there is to see and then go home," said Polo.

"There's nothing to see here," the Matriarch said with a sigh. "There are just rocks, sand, parched earth and unremitting heat… though the heat has been less intense lately. We know every inch of The Oven. We knew you were coming long before you came, and you can take from me that there is nothing else worth seeing."

"You could show them the scrolls," a very young-looking shrew, who had remained silent up to this point, said.

"You had better go and get them," the Matriarch said without enthusiasm.

After he disappeared, the Matriarch added: "I don't know why he brought that up, but you might as well have a look while you are here."

The young shrew quickly returned with two pieces of rolled-up parchment and laid them out flat on the floor. One featured a picture of a being similar to the one on the scrolls Marcus had found on the earlier expedition. The other was of a middle-aged mouse in military uniform with a pawful of medals attached to the tunic.

"I have got one almost exactly like that!" Marcus exclaimed after looking at the former. "It has the same mysterious mammal, and the words to the side look the same as well. They're the same length, anyway." Marcus was able to see that the top word began with the letter H, while the lower, longer one ended with an S.

Marcus looked long and hard at this scroll, before turning his attention to the other one. "This one is new to me," he said. "It rings no bells at all."

The Matriarch reacted to this observation with rage. "How dare you?!" she spluttered, with eyes so red that the whites could not be seen. "Why do you think we hate you so?!" She then momentarily turned on the youngster who had unearthed the scrolls. "Why did you have to bring this up?! You must have known it would have got me going?!" The youngster trembled and offered an abject apology.

The Matriarch glared at Marcus. "I was beginning to think you were intelligent!" she said. "But you are not! You don't understand! You are just stupid, stupid, stupid!"

"Perhaps you could enlighten us?" Rosencrantz suggested.

After a minute's silence, during which a pin could have been heard to drop, the Matriarch said in more measured tones: "Perhaps I should. The picture on the scroll is of one of the top generals who took part in the big mouse takeover. I am talking of the time when the mice on the island first became all-powerful and crushed all opposition in the process."

She paused to look at Rosencrantz and say: "The gerbils did not fare well in this," and then at Boxer, who was told: "The hamsters had a hard time, too."

"So, what exactly happened?" Marcus asked. "Why are you so bitter?"

The Matriarch snorted again. "You really don't get it, do you?" she said with a sneer. "All right, I will explain."

"The general on that piece of parchment was one of the so-called mouse heroes. He earned his medals for the ruthless way he helped to crush all rodents that might be seen as a threat to mouse supremacy. He and other generals conducted a campaign of oppression that included murder, rape, beatings, torture and imprisonment without trial."

"Did the shrews suffer more than other rodents?" Marcus asked. "There are still plenty of gerbils and hamsters around but no shrews."

"The reason for that is very simple. The shrews put up a fight. They resisted. So, too, did the rats and voles, I believe. Shrews don't like to be bullied. It is in our nature to fight back... not like the lily-livered gerbils and hamsters!"

"I'm not lily-livered, and I don't like being called a coward!" an angry Boxer protested.

"I'm none too keen on that notion either!" Rosencrantz added.

That made the Matriarch laugh. "All right, perhaps you're not!" she said. "But you're straying from the point.

"The shrew population was decimated. Those who weren't bumped off by those heavily armed mouse soldiers – who undoubtedly thought they were brave – were driven out of towns and forced to live in remote locations where they hoped they would not be found. But, even then, they were not safe. They continued to be hunted down and, when caught, put on trial for something and then executed in public. Other rodents, including gerbils and hamsters, were often paid for information leading to their capture."

"I never knew it was as bad as that," said Polo. "I remember, as a youngster, seeing the occasional shrew around but never got to know any of them and, to be honest, never thought about them. But then, I was very young."

"That's honest, if nothing else," the Matriarch conceded. "I now hope you have some idea of why we were less than delighted to see you turning up at The Oven."

"I'm glad to have met you," said Marcus. "I have learned from you, and I hope you won't mind if I write something about our meeting when I get home. I am a journalist at the *Phoenix Standard* and one of the main reasons I am on this expedition is to write about it. We are no longer war-like, and I believe the public should be made aware of the truth."

"You'd better not be war-like!" the Matriarch snarled. "There may not be many of us, but we are well armed and prepared to withstand any form of attack. We also know every nook and cranny of our territory."

Marcus made one last attempt to establish a working relationship with the Matriarch and the other shrews. "Are you sure I can't persuade you to come back with us to Phoenix and spend a little time there? If you can't come, perhaps one of the others could?"

He knew he was treading on thin ice, and he received the reaction he both feared and expected.

"You really like to push your luck, don't you?!" the Matriarch replied, with all the redness back in her eyes. "You have had your answer already… and it is *no*! Now get out of here, all of you, and go back the way you came before we do you a mischief!"

There was nothing for it but to withdraw immediately. Once out of earshot, Marcus said to his companions: "That was quite an experience! I can't wait to write about it!" Then he added: "However, in spite of what the Matriarch said to the contrary, there might still be more interesting things for us to look at… though I personally suspect that there probably isn't." He asked the others what they thought.

Rosencrantz and Boxer both looked at Marcus… and then at Polo, who was seen to be wheezing and gasping for breath again. "I'm really sorry, but I'm not feeling so good," the great explorer said in a pitch that was unusually high for him. "I haven't felt entirely right for some time. All I want to do is go home. You can take it from me that if I am not in the mood for exploring, there must be something seriously wrong with me! I am sorrier than I can say if I'm spoiling things for everyone else."

As the quartet made their way back to the Flying Machine, they became aware of a dramatic change in the weather. The temperature dropped, and then there was a gale that blew sand into eyes, noses, mouths and throats. A huge cloud appeared from nowhere and a fork of lightning lit up the sky. A deafening thunderclap followed, and there were more than a few drops of rain. The drop in temperature, if nothing else, was welcome.

Polo was becoming increasingly poorly, though, and it soon became necessary for Boxer to carry him. In the conditions that prevailed, that was no easy task, and even the mighty Boxer was breathing heavily long before the explorers reached their transport.

Marcus and Rosencrantz expressed amazement in unison when they saw that the Flying Machine was surrounded by puddles. However, the machine proved to still be in good working order. Marcus and Rosencrantz climbed aboard, while Boxer gently placed Polo onto a back seat and sat beside him.

By then, however, the legendary explorer's heavy breathing had ceased, and it soon became apparent why. The journey home was a sombre one and made in silence.

Marcus contemplated the fact that he, in particular, could expect a hero's welcome once the Flying Machine had touched down in Phoenix. He was far from sure he could be receptive to such a welcome.

CHAPTER 25

Brass bands, bunting and a battery of well-wishers awaited the return of the intrepid quartet. The latter included the Prime Minister, the Chairman of the Board and a jaded-looking Da Vinci. Phaedra was at the front, too, and as soon as Marcus alighted from the Flying Machine, she embraced him passionately with the words, "You're my hero!"

The rapturous reception soon quietened, however, when news of Polo's death filtered through. Arrangements had been made to take his body to the morgue and, once it had been taken away, Da Vinci invited Marcus, Rosencrantz and Boxer to join him in his workshop.

"You must be tired," Da Vinci said to them. "I should imagine that the last thing you want is to be beleaguered by crowds." The gratitude expressed was genuine. However, Marcus could not fail to notice that Da Vinci looked extremely tired himself. *How much longer can the island rely on him for making marvellous inventions?* he wondered. Several hours of animated conversation followed nonetheless, before everyone had a nap where they sat, and the three travellers departed.

* * *

Everyone wanted to shake Marcus's paw on the day he returned to the office. The 'mouse of the moment' had spent two days 'chilling out' at home and was now ready to be back in the public eye. As he entered the newsroom, there were loud cheers. Phaedra hugged and kissed him once more, and Gertrude followed suit before the others in the room queued to congratulate him. Even Adonis was effusive in his praise.

The final handshake was followed by a request, via Gertrude, for Marcus to see the Chairman of the Board.

"I trust you have had a good chance to recover from the rigours of your amazing new expedition?" the Chairman asked from behind his desk.

"Yes, I have, thank you, though the death of Polo has taken away some of the gloss of the experience," Marcus replied from the other side.

"I appreciate that," the Chairman said. "I understand Polo died from a respiratory condition that had existed for years but not been detected. He must go down as a legend in our time, and it is only fitting for the *Standard* to pay the full cost of the funeral. The funeral will, of course, be a high-profile one, and we will pay the cost of the wake afterwards as well."

"That's good to hear," said Marcus. "He was quite a cult figure on the island, and I have always had immense respect for him."

The Chairman, in his unvarying monotone, said: "Me too." Marcus looked for a flicker of emotion once more, but there was none.

"However, that is not the reason I asked you to come and

see me," the Chairman then said. "I am going to have to make some editorial changes at the *Standard*, and they involve you.

"Caxton has had a serious mental breakdown, as you know, and he won't be coming back for a long time – if ever – and I need to appoint a new Editor."

Marcus's heart missed a beat.

"We have also lost Iago," the Chairman continued. "He tried to undermine Caxton's authority while here, and I didn't like the way he conducted himself generally. He is totally charmless and lacks the personality to be a newspaper figurehead. He and I had a disagreement, and he has left the paper."

"That leaves two holes to fill. Do you know what Iago is doing now?"

"I hear he has moved to the *Troy Courier*. They are having financial difficulties there, I'm told, and they have brought in Iago as a hatchet mouse. Just the right job for him, perhaps!"

The Chairman then paused, and Marcus knew what was coming next.

"As you know, Caxton had, and probably still has, tremendous charisma," he continued. "Along with Da Vinci and, until recently, Polo, he has, for years, been seen as one of the Andronicus icons. His departure leaves a massive gap, and I need another mouse with charisma to fill that gap."

"Does such a mouse exist?"

"I think you know the answer to that. The two expeditions you have been on have transformed you into a cult figure in your own right. Your name is on everyone's lips everywhere. What you have accomplished is amazing. This is especially so because, although you had no previous exploring experience, you were able to take over as leader on each trip. The *Standard* needs leadership, too. And, if that's not enough, you have personality. There was a time when, to be frank, you didn't. But you do now! Your self-confidence has grown out of all recognition."

"If you are offering me the chance to lead the editorial team at the *Standard*… with your help, of course… I will gladly accept," said Marcus.

"That's excellent!" the Chairman said. "There were two candidates I had in mind for the job, and you were my first choice. The other candidate, as you will have undoubtedly guessed, was Phaedra. She has personality, too, and I would like her to be your deputy. Are you happy with that?"

Marcus confirmed that he was, knowing full well that it made no difference if he wasn't.

"While you were away, Phaedra wrote a splendid 'Personality' article about Polo," the Chairman added. "She has written another fine piece following his untimely death. She should strengthen the rodent-interest element in the paper."

Marcus marvelled at the way the Chairman could come quickly to the point and say what he wanted to say without wasting his own time. He asked the Chairman for his thoughts on appointing a new Features Editor, following Phaedra's promotion.

"Make your own choice," he was told. "That can be your first executive decision!"

"One idea might be to appoint Cicero, who is extremely experienced and knowledgeable, to the post and train someone else up to replace him when he retires… which will be quite soon."

The reply, with a shrug, of 'up to you' signalled the end of the conversation.

Phaedra was waiting outside as he left. She brushed past him, tapped him on the shoulder and, with a wink, said: "See you later!"

Marcus's first job as Editor was to get Titus to organise comprehensive coverage of Polo's funeral, along with providing details of his life and achievements. His second task was to track down Cicero and his third, he decided on a whim, was to place a bet on the latest dog race and ensure that his prediction appeared in the paper.

He had put his money on a rank outsider but had become so accurate and confident with his predictions that he was sure plenty of money would come his way, as well as kudos. In the event, the outsider trailed in last and the new Editor of the *Phoenix Standard* and master forecaster felt deflated for the first time for as long as he could remember.

However, the funeral of Polo was the grand affair that Marcus, along with everyone else, had expected. Mourners attended from all over the island and the cortege to the graveyard was the longest ever seen. Marcus, Rosencrantz and Boxer were a prominent part of it, of course.

Mourners present at the most lavish of wakes included Caxton. Looking pale and drawn and with no hint of his celebrated smile, he had kept out of the public eye for a long time and, at the wake, he kept to himself. Conspicuous by his absence was Da Vinci, who had said he was feeling under the weather.

Marcus was feeling vaguely out of sorts, too. He did not feel unwell physically, but he did not feel quite himself... not his new self, anyway.

After an unsuccessful attempt to buttonhole Caxton, find out how he was and perhaps find out something new to put in the *Standard*, Marcus decided to leave the wake early and look up Da Vinci.

"I'm really sorry to have missed it," the fabled inventor told him as he sat slumped in a chair close to the Flying Machine. "Unfortunately, I haven't felt up to much lately, and my doctor has advised me to retire. I have a heart condition, apparently, and the doc says it's imperative for me to rest."

Marcus could see that Da Vinci had aged even since the last time he saw him. "I hope it will still be possible to see you... I mean, as a friend and not just to interview you... and then write something for the *Standard*," he said, after making the right sympathetic noises.

"Of course you can," said Da Vinci. "You are welcome to write something for the newspaper and you can call any time. I will be going away for a bit but still plan to spend time in my workshop after that... if only to rest!"

"That's marvellous!" said Marcus, who had always been flattered by the fact that he was one of the few rodents around who Da Vinci had time for. "I will never forget the way you let me travel in your Flying Machine."

"You can go up in it any time you like," Da Vinci assured him. "I might even bequeath it to the *Standard* one day."

Marcus was genuinely surprised, and he faltered before saying: "Thank you. I did not expect that."

Da Vinci gave a weary chuckle. "Now you have taken *me* by surprise!" he said. "Anyway, as you can see, I am feeling a little tired and would like to be left alone just now."

Marcus mumbled his thanks and promised to be in touch again soon, before heading back to his new workstation.

The Editor's office was made to look even bigger than it actually was by its emptiness. Before Caxton's departure, it had been filled with books, albums, family photographs and various forms of memorabilia unrelated to the *Phoenix Standard*. Now, there were just three photographs on the wall and, on the main desk, a telephone, a large diary, three wire trays containing paperwork and a trophy won for the *Standard* by Adonis and others a few years ago.

Just after Marcus sat down and began to consult the diary, the telephone rang and he found himself talking to Gertrude, the news desk secretary. "Cicero is here to see you," she told him. Marcus, who had forgotten that this was the day that he was due to return, asked her to send him in.

"Well, well, well! How times have changed!" Cicero said as he breezed in. "And how *you* have changed! I have always said that nothing is constant, but, even so, heartiest congratulations on your promotion!"

Marcus had never seen the veteran Feature Writer in such effervescent form. "Never mind that, how are *you*? I have been trying to contact you for ages."

"I have been receiving treatment for cancer," Cicero said in a tone that was still nothing less than upbeat. "I had been feeling unwell for some time. I had some tests and, once the diagnosis was made, I received all the necessary treatment. This put me out of action for some time, of course. But now I am back! I'm as fit and firing as ever!"

"It's good to see you back," Marcus assured him. "Apart from anything else, I need someone like you in my corner. Would you like to be Features Editor?"

"I would be delighted, but as you know, I am due to retire in just over a year. Wouldn't you be better off with someone younger?"

"I have thought about that, and I would like you to train

someone up to take over once you go. You can help me find a potential successor."

"That's great, thank you very much!" said Cicero. "One thing's for sure: life at the *Standard* will never be the same again. I can't imagine, at the moment, what it will be like without a Caxton or an Iago."

"Yes, especially Caxton. He's been more than a journalist. He has been the face of the newspaper, an island icon."

"Now, there's a thought," said Cicero. "Until recently, there were three icons… Caxton being one of them. One of the other two has sadly died, and the third has reportedly given up inventing."

"That could be something for you to write about," said Marcus. "The three great icons and who, if anyone, will replace them?"

"Another thing's for sure," said Cicero. "Nothing is constant… as I'm sure you have heard me say before!"

Marcus, who had heard him say that countless times, said the climate seemed to be changing, too.

"I have always said that climate change was on the way, and I have no doubt in my mind that I am being proved right… almost as we speak," said Cicero. "Nothing is constant!"

"You can write about that, too," said Marcus. "There is now evidence to back your opinion up."

"I would also like to write about 'The Origins of Mousekind' once more," said Cicero. "The scrolls that you managed to unearth provide a bit of concrete evidence that another race of beings was in charge of the island before the rise of the rodent."

"I am hoping it will be possible to go back to where I

found the scrolls and that giant book and bring back the book and various other things I was not able to carry then," said Marcus. "I would, in fact, like to retrace the steps I made on both my expeditions and see what else can be found. When I can find the time to do so, is open to conjecture, of course."

"One thing I can guarantee is that you will learn something new if you do," said Cicero.

"Like what?"

"You might learn more about the super race that ruled before mice took over. I have no doubt that there was such a race. The mystery is what wiped it out. I personally believe the cause was a holocaust of some sort. I also think there could be another one on the way, perhaps sooner than we think. If there is one, will mice become extinct, too, I wonder? Will another kind of rodent take over? Or will birds or butterflies be in charge? Or perhaps ladybirds? Nothing is constant!"

"Those are interesting thoughts, though I can't help thinking your imagination is running riot a bit!" Marcus said diplomatically.

"Yes, I suppose it is!" Cicero conceded. "There's just one other thing, though," he said gravely. "I gather your latest bet went awry. Are you losing your touch as a forecaster? Perhaps the effects of the dust that got into your system during your first expedition are wearing off. Perhaps I am right, after all, about nothing being constant!"

CHAPTER 26

"What do you think about the changing sky?" Titus asked Marcus on the telephone.

"What about it?" Marcus replied.

"It's gone a funny colour, don't you think?" asked Titus. "Is there anything in particular you would like us to write on the subject?"

Marcus, who had not entered the newsroom during the three days that followed his official appointment as Editor, told Titus to use his judgement. "Do what you think is best," he said.

The new Editor, who had not looked at the sky for three days, had other things on his mind. One was the question of which of his belongings he should put in his office to make it look more homely.

The other concerned the choice of candidate on the council. A vacancy had arisen following a sudden resignation, and Titus had asked Marcus to use his fabled powers of prediction and name the replacement in advance. Marcus had no idea who it might be at all, but he named someone anyway and was spectacularly wrong.

He knew that, sooner or later, he would have to show his face and admit, tacitly anyway, that even an editor can be fallible. Eventually, he decided it was time to stop fretting, visit the newsroom and have a chat with Cicero, if nothing else. But he got that wrong, too. "I'm afraid Cicero's not here," Gertrude told him. "He suddenly felt unwell a while ago and had to go home."

Titus looked up from his desk and told Marcus he had got someone to write about the dramatically changing sky. "That's excellent!" said Marcus, who seemed to be talking on autopilot.

The new Editor thought it might be an idea to touch base with Phaedra, his deputy, to discuss future plans for the newspaper. When he asked where he could find her, Gertrude gave him a curious look before saying: "I believe she's with the Chairman in his office." Marcus hurriedly left the newsroom, oblivious to whispers among the reporters.

Back in his office, he decided to telephone Cicero. "I'm terribly sorry, but I'm not feeling so good," the latter said. "I have a feeling that the old trouble has come back." Cicero then asked Marcus how he was settling into his new job.

Marcus replied that everything was fine. "Don't worry about me!" he said.

Marcus was about to tell Cicero not to return to work until he was fully recovered, when the features veteran changed the subject by asking: "What do you think about the weather? The sky is looking really strange at the moment." On putting the receiver down, Marcus realised it was high time he had a look for himself.

To say that the sky looked strange was an understatement. It was red, restless-looking and angry. The shades of red changed intermittently, and Marcus could see in the distance what looked like volcanic embers being thrown upwards from inside, or just outside, The Oven. A bolt of lightning was barely visible against its backdrop, but the thunder that followed it was so tumultuous that the entire island seemed to shake in its wake.

The island shuddered a second time without any obvious help from the sky, and the sky then began to turn grey... and then black. As the sky darkened, Marcus could see gigantic flames many miles away. Parts of the island were on fire, and Marcus strongly suspected that the areas he could not see were engulfed by flames as well.

A ferocious wind followed and began to whip up the flames into an even greater frenzy. The temperature remained unseasonably mild, but Marcus still shuddered. A second thunderclap shook the island even more than the first, and Marcus stood there mesmerised by the magnitude of what had happened. Then, the wind suddenly dropped, and stillness reigned for an hour or so.

The lull was a prelude to a storm of cataclysmic proportions, followed by hour upon hour of rain that fell like one giant waterfall. There followed a period when there was no wind or rain, though the sky became a menacing, unremitting red once more.

Marcus treated this second lull as an opportunity to go outside and look around. He saw that low-lying areas had been flooded, though much of the floodwater was disappearing into drains that were there to cope with the Wet Season.

He helped himself to a *Standard* buggy and headed for the coast and the cliff tops... where the biggest surprise of all awaited him.

The sea had completely disappeared. All that lay in front of Marcus was an endless expanse of sand, pebbles, rocks, seaweed, a few rock pools and the carcasses of fish and other creatures Marcus had never seen before. With the aid of a telescope, he discovered that this sealess expanse stretched for miles.

On the horizon, however, there was a small bump, which could conceivably be another island. Marcus wondered whether the island, if that was what it was, compared in size with the Isle of Andronicus. And was there any life on it? And, if so, was it ruled by rodents or some other form of life?

Marcus did his best to study the bump, but there were no clues. Eventually, it disappeared, having been enveloped by what looked like a mist. After several minutes, the mist looked more like a wall and, after a little longer, the wall seemed to be sighing. The sighs grew louder as the wall became ever larger, until it even eclipsed the skyline.

After a while longer, there was no doubt that the wall was moving towards Andronicus. It was a wall of water, and everything in its path disappeared. It was ceasing to sigh and was instead giving out an almighty roar that became louder by the second.

Marcus, who had for some time been reconciled to the loss of his physic powers, had no difficulty in predicting what would happen next. He knew that he should flee for his life but instead remained where he was… transfixed and utterly mesmerised.

By the time the wall had got close to the cliffs, the roar was deafening and the top of it could not be seen. The cliffs were so dwarfed that they resembled a garden rockery.

Everything in the wall's path was enveloped. The entire Isle of Andronicus was overcome by a seething, salty mass.

Even the spitting protests from The Oven and the island's volcanoes were extinguished without ceremony. No part of the island was spared.

The effects of the subsequent undertow were equally devastating. All mouse-made structures, including the homes on stilts, were demolished and pulled towards the cliffs and thrown to the bottom of them. The surface of the island was exposed for a while, until the tide returned. Most of the surface was now a mass of mud, on which lay fallen trees, debris and dead bodies. Mile upon mile, even in deserted areas, was dominated by the smell of death.

* * *

After barely a day, another wall of water arrived… and brought with it a new order of life on the Isle of Andronicus.

A shoal of sardines appeared, with the clear intention of making their presence felt in a habitat that now offered a variety of saltwater and freshwater outlets. The sardine leader was Archimedes, a massive specimen with gimlet eyes, razor-like teeth and scales that acted like shields.

"This is where we can hold sway," the leader said to his first lieutenant. "What sort of opposition have we got?" The lieutenant made mention of possible freshwater rivals.

"That's a point," said Archimedes, "we still have the might of the minnows to contend with."